A Pool, A Suitor, A Cellist
Bright Shadows Series:
Novelette Trilogies for Busy Folks

By R. Manolakas

Trilogy One

I0557863

Contents

Dedication and Quote

Dedication: This book is dedicated to my mother and father—Mrs Betty Manolakas and the late Dr George S. Manolakas, and to the late Rod Serling, whose writing provided countless hours of imaginative entertainment.

Quote: "Fair is foul—and foul is fair."—Shakespeare's *Macbeth*

Introduction

This is the first volume of a series of strange trilogies, each volume containing three novelettes. Each small novel (presented in three handy parts) is about three to four times as long as the typical short story, and about one seventh as long as the standard novel. Nevertheless, they contain enough sub-plots, characters, and complications to delight a listener, reader, or film patron. They are, both text and audio versions, designed to entertain busy folks who want a nice slice of riveting fiction that they can consume in "one sitting," whether on a plane, in a car, or riding an exercise bike. They are meant to satisfy the current appetite for "binge reading."

Most of us lead rather frantic lives these days, and the stress and time pressure makes us reluctant to add time consuming assignments to our already tight schedules. Hopefully, the tales that follow do not seem like tasks, but rather handy indulgences of your hungry imaginations—that are both entertaining and fulfilling.

Years ago, I watched the TV series *Twilight Zone*, *One Step Beyond*, and *The Outer Limits* because they contained short, spine-tingling stories that were strange yet identifiable—*they could almost happen.* I hope you get that same feeling from this book. R. M. 4/2014.

Prologue

Our first story, set in contemporary southern California in an upscale suburb, concerns an ordinary piece of plumbing in a rather ordinary swimming pool. What happens to the intelligent, pretty, eight-year-old girl isn't ordinary, however. A window appears into her world that comes around maybe once in a millennium—or perhaps more often to those who believe?

Our second tale is set in pre-WWI Munich, Germany, and involves a love story—of sorts. It's hard to believe that only one century has passed since the beginning of the First World War, which many believe set the stage for the Second. That century presented unimaginable slaughter and cruelty. The shy, prim young man in our story who courts the lovely young lady is very single-minded and determined—but about what? You may be surprised to know.

Our last tale dangles between the shadows and crevices of our minds, exploring the connections between our senses, the sensual, and extra-sensory experiences, and how they interplay with the "rational" world. Salvation is a topic that has consumed humankind for thousands of years, and it comes wrapped in all kinds of packages, no matter what one's spiritual beliefs are. What's one person's burden can also become a redemption, spinning chance on its head. Decide for yourself.

One caveat—please don't read the Epilogue before you read the novelettes. May all your shadows be bright ones, and please look for the next trilogy in the series that should be out soon.

Novelette One: A Pool
Part One:

Dr Harvey Black and his eight-year-old daughter hiked in the brown hills behind their suburban home, enjoying the view of the Saddleback Valley on a hot Labour Day weekend. Rebecca busied herself with a stone that she had discovered along the bushy path.

He glanced at his daughter across the narrow trail. "Be careful doll, there might be snakes." Harvey's sad, brown eyes fastened upon the glittery object in her hands. He removed his Tilley hat from his sweaty, balding head. "Let's have a look at what you found."

Rebecca, a tall girl for her age, pushed the spray of golden hair from her high, rounded forehead and penetrating blue-green eyes as she held up the object, "It's a gift—just for us, Father."

She moved closer to him, her long tanned legs shooting out from under her pink shorts, deftly navigating the crevices and little rocks dotting the trail. "A beautiful gift," Rebecca announced as she handed him the curiosity, "it's from *her*."

The little girl gazed at her father with an intensity that suggested thoughts far beyond his ken.

"*Her*? Who do you mean?" asked Harvey.

He had always felt that his daughter's voice was unusually smooth and assured for a little girl, and at times it made him feel uncomfortable.

"The Water Lady," she answered.

Harvey remembered. His daughter had taken up the fiction of a mystical lady living under the drain in their swimming pool.

He took the strange object in his hand and shook his head, speaking in a halting, whispery voice that seemed dusted off and sparingly used.

"Looks like quartz," he said as he felt its sharp edges.

"Isn't it pretty?"

"Yes, dear, it is."

He pushed back the few stands of the light brown hair that he had left and placed his hat back on.

"You can keep it, I suppose. Put it in your pocket. Don't tell your mother, though."

He glanced at his brown-rimmed, oval watch, the precious memento left to him by his late father. "Mommy's done swimming. Let's get back."

Harvey's gold wedding band glistened in the sun as he waved Rebecca on. "You can take a dip too. It's hot."

Dr Black headed for their back yard over the crest of the hill as Rebecca prattled about the Water Lady. What an imagination little girls have, thought Harvey. The Water Lady had left the stone just for them. The Water Lady was going away after Thanksgiving, though, and so forth. Good, thought Harvey, none too soon.

He used to have an active imagination like that too, he lamented, but life's trials and stresses had extinguished it.

Or, was it just beneath the surface instead?

They hiked up the hill and into the back yard of their California, ranch-style home that bordered the canyon, with a sweeping view of the valley. A cool, sparkling, blue-green pool promised entertainment and refreshment.

Harvey sat under the shade of an umbrella that rested upon the Mexican tile deck. He smelled the jasmine that dotted the perimeter of the yard.

Rebecca peeled off her shorts and tank top, down to her red, two-piece bathing suit and pink, bootie socks. She stepped into the large pool with her glitter-rimmed, swimming goggles. Like her mother, the little girl was trim and fit—quite the tomboy.

As usual, she was careful not to disturb Mrs. Black's workout when her busy mother swam her laps. Nevertheless, her mother stopped swimming, standing up in the shallow end. She removed her goggles and bathing cap with a hint of irritation, glancing at her daughter as one might eye an intruder.

Rachael looked up at her husband resting under the umbrella, next to the big, green, full-leafed maple tree. It seemed as out of place—next to the line of swaying palms—as a totem pole.

"I see you're back already," said Mrs. Black dryly.

"She found another pretty stone, Rachael."

Her large, hazel eyes darted with a hawk's vigilance. "I'm so thrilled."

Rebecca dove to the drain at the deep end of the pool. Her mother stepped out of the pool and cornered her husband on the deck.

"Why aren't you working today?"

Also a doctor—an oncologist—she liked to speak frankly. She threw her voice out in cool waves whose force diminished, as it advanced, rather like breakers crashing upon the rocks. A lean and angular young woman, with a perfectly straight nose and straight blond hair, she sported a head-turning figure with nothing out of place—just like her hair.

"I spoke with Dr. Milford again—the Medical Director of the clinic," said Harvey.

"And . . .?"

She stood over Harvey with her perfectly manicured hands placed rigidly upon her narrow hips, the lavender sparkle of her nail polish playing with the sun.

"He sort of cornered me."

"What happened?"

He let out a sigh, his troubled eyes shifting from his daughter's dives to his wife's intense stare.

"I told Milford I wanted to spend more time with my family."

"Can't you even *try* to cooperate with Dr. Milford?" Her voice hardened. "He wants to promote you to a management position, too."

Harvey shrugged. "You give this guy an inch and he takes a—"

"—A *mile*! Right—why not *give* him a mile?"

She pointed to herself. "*I* do. That clinic I work in is a hellhole! I put out because we need the *extras* in life."

Her tight, black swimsuit hugged her toned body even more as she adjusted the straps.

Harvey's eyes shifted back to the pool.

"We've been over this Rachael . . ." His eyes scanning the surface of the pool, he noticed that there was no Rebecca. His gaze shot to the bottom of the pool. Terror gripped him.

The blurred red figure at the drain didn't budge. The small pink feet didn't move either.

"Rebecca!" he screamed.

Harvey dove into the pool and straight to his daughter, who was lying near the drain. He dragged her up to the surface.

By the time he emerged, Rachael had dived into the water too. "My God! Put her on the deck!" she screamed.

Churning his legs as hard as he could, Harvey rushed Rebecca through the shallow end with Rachael close behind. He felt Rebecca's arms and legs moving in his arms—a thankful sign! Rushing up the steps, he placed his daughter down gently upon the warm deck.

Rebecca tore off her goggles. She giggled.

"What on earth were you doing down there?" demanded Harvey as he crouched over his daughter. "I thought you had drowned."

"How dare you scare us to death!" screamed Rachael, her face red as she stood on the deck, glaring down at Rebecca. "This isn't funny."

She yanked the little girl up off the tiles. "Answer your father!"

"I visited the Water Lady again, the pretty lady under the drain. I'm all right, really I am."

Harvey stood up, "Well, no harm done I guess," he said softly, his eyes avoiding his wife's.

Rachael grabbed Rebecca's shoulders and shook her hard. "I told you not to dive to the drain any more!"

The little girl pushed her away. "The Water Lady wants us to be together again!" Her eyes shifted between her parents. "Don't you want that?"

"Get inside!" shouted Rachael.

Rebecca started to cry, and then ran into the house. Harvey watched her leave. "She meant no harm."

"What the hell did she mean, 'together again'?" Rachael glared at her husband. "We're together *now*. Well, aren't we Harvey?"

"I think . . . I know what she means."

Harvey followed his daughter into the house.

"I want that too—more than anything," he whispered sadly.

Rachael, having oiled and scented her body, slid into the wide, king-sized bed under the white, Egyptian cotton sheets. Harvey, in his brown flannel pajamas, studied his journal.

Lying in bed with her back to her husband, she grabbed her smart phone off the bed-stand texted.

"How's your article?" she asked him flatly.

"Fine."

He glanced over at her tanned and lovely back, partially covered by the sheer nightie.

Their spacious master bedroom, appointed in neutral, cream-colored furniture and bare, white walls, lulled the senses. A picture window view of the sweeping Saddleback Valley—alight with the twinkling of the houses sitting lower in the valley—offered a potentially stimulating exception.

"She does that a lot, you know?" said Rachael as she tapped her phone buttons.

"Who?"

"Your daughter."

"Does what?"

"Dives to the drain in the pool."

"She's probably seeing how long she can hold her breath. I used to do that what I was a kid."

"You mean before your nasal problems?" Rachael yawned, "*You* know what she's always doing down there—talking to that mythical *woman* again. Can't you ever face facts, Harvey?"

Harvey took off his reading glasses and plopped his journal on the nightstand. "She's just a little girl with an imagination."

"*Too* good. There's something's wrong with Rebecca," she added with an icy finality.

"Oh, come on." He scooted over in the bed closer to his wife who was busy studying her phone. "Let's enjoy the view, honey." He glanced out the window. "I'm sorry about my work."

Rachael kept texting.

He put his hand gently upon her smooth shoulder, which looked even more tanned against the pure white silk of her nightie.

"Sure thing."

"Who are you texting?"

"Dr. Navarro, the child psychiatrist. I trained with her. She's good—and sees adults too. Poor lady, her son died a year ago—a weird accident."

"Rebecca doesn't need to see a shrink."

She threw her cell phone down and turned out the light.

"The hell she doesn't."

Harvey scooted back over in bed, pulling the covers around him.

"She may . . . kill herself . . . doing things like that," said Rachael darkly.

When Harvey woke up early the following morning, his wife had already left for work. He heard a muffled voice behind the wall next to him, coming from Rebecca's bedroom. He got out of bed and padded down the hallway.

"Can we really live with you?" he heard his daughter ask as he put his ear to her bedroom door. "It's beautiful there," she continued. "It's happy, too."

Rebecca is alone in there, he reassured himself. Is she talking to herself again?

He knocked gently upon the door. "Rebecca? Are you all right?" With no answer, Harvey tried the knob. It was unlocked. He gently pushed the door open.

His daughter sat up in bed in her long, red T-shirt, holding a black onyx stone in her hand as if she were conversing with it. "See my new friend?" She held up the stone.

"I heard you talking to someone . . . well, never mind," said Harvey. He entered the room and walked over to her bed.

He knew enough pediatrics to understand that conversing with mythical characters—let alone a rock—was a bit unusual for such an intelligent eight-year-old child.

"You *know* who it was, Father."

Harvey sat down on the bed next to his daughter.

"What's that in your hand, Rebecca?"

"Another rock."

"I know honey, but where did you get it?"

He scanned the un-girlish appointments of her sparsely furnished, earth-toned room, including three unframed posters on the sand-colored walls.

Two prints featured pictures of vast, blue-green seas—one with a setting sun over it and one with frolicking dolphins—the third a photo of a smiling and youthful Albert Einstein.

"It's my present from the Water Lady. The earth stone is part of her spirit."

She held up the shiny black object. "She wants me to come away with her."

Harvey looked down at the long, rectangular, black clothes-chest—another oddity.

"Where to?"

"Under the pool—and into the deep blue water," she replied. "I've seen it there. It's lovely—so colorful and calm. I told mother about it too."

"Calm?"

"*Peaceful*—I'm going to live there."

The bewildered father stood up and looked through the child's window to the pool deck outside, his eyes landing upon the huge, leafy maple tree. It already had a few yellow leaves with the cooling nights.

"Get dressed, dear. Let's have breakfast. Maybe we can watch the football game afterwards."

"Goodie!"

He smiled at the childish reply. It reassured him, but only a little. Something was wrong, he thought, terribly wrong. Perhaps Rachael was right, he thought.

"You see the disc bulge at L-four, that's pinching on the nerve root in the lumbar spine . . ."

Harvey, attired in his long, white lab coat, dress shirt, dark slacks, and tie pointed with his pencil to the greyish blob on the MRI film. A similarly attired young intern stood next to him in the radiology office, observing the film on a bright view-box that hung on the wall.

Harvey's eyes shot to the portly, sixtyish Medical Director—Dr. Milford—bursting into the room.

"Doctor Black, may I have a word please?"

Milford drew him aside.

"What's this I hear about you turning down extra call?"

Harvey cleared his throat.

"I'm having, ah . . . some issues at home—"

"—I don't want to hear it."

"But . . ."

Milford took a hankie from his coat pocket and cleaned off his eyeglasses as he examined the lenses. "Your work is good, Dr. Black, your work is very good, but you must work *harder*, you must work *longer.*"

Harvey's eyes fastened upon Milford's white carnation that adorned the lapel of his dark, pinstriped suit. "Yes, Dr. Milford."

"You must *work, work, and work.*" Milford waved his fist in rhythm with the repeating words.

"Yes Dr. Milford, but you see—"

"—Look Black, the suits in the corner office say this HMO's not profitable. To stay here, you need to advance, understand? The assistant directorship could be yours."

"Yes, but I'm happy with—"

"—*Impossible*, understand? If I pick you, you need to *double* your hours. Nothing stays the same. You advance, or you go."

"Yes, but my daughter and wife—"

"—You must advance, or you go."

"I'm happy—"

"—You've got three months to prove yourself Black, understand? Don't let me down. We need to triple our outpatient visits and quadruple our rate of testing . . ."

Harvey looked over at the intern who met his glance, then the young man quickly looked away, obviously embarrassed.

Harvey tried to talk over his boss. "My daughter needs—"

"—Impossible."

Satisfied that the lenses were spotless, Milford donned his glasses, finishing his monologue. "Any questions?" He didn't wait for an answer. "In short, you advance, or—"

Harvey filled in the rest: "—Or, *I go*."

Milford looked at him doubtfully.

"Right—enjoyed our chat, Black."

"See this? Rebecca's painting—for my class—good, is it not?"

Harvey stared at the alluring, black rectangle that his child had painted in watercolor, wondering where he had seen the object before.

The tiny, ancient woman with the withered skin and diagonal scar across her cheek put the picture down upon her tidy, imitation-mahogany desk.

"Rebecca is very beautiful, Doctor," the teacher's eyes radiated warmth. "Yes, beautiful."

Harvey sat in the empty, third grade classroom with Rebecca's teacher, Pearl Nguyen. Rumor had it that her scar had been a parting gift from communist insurgents that had overrun her small Vietnamese village in the mid-seventies.

Rachael demanded that he attend the parent-teacher conferences, and he did so this time with trepidation, since Pearl had called the meeting in haste. As they sat across from each other, Harvey glanced out the window at the hard rain pinging against the glass, his eyes moving to a lovely, brown stone resting upon her desk.

Pearl noted his interest. "You like?"

Harvey nodded. "It's nice."

She picked up the rock and handed it to him. "Feel."

He felt it. He noted its odd warmth.

"Yes, do not be afraid." She laid it back on her desk. "Energy, earth-energy makes heat."

"You wanted to see me about something?"

The rich but cracking voice of the teacher took on a somber tone.

"Yes, it is true. When I was a young girl in Vietnam, in our village, a little girl lived there who was much like Rebecca. This child was very special."

Harvey could hear the pinging of the rain against the window getting louder.

"*Special*? How do you mean?"

Pearl took the brown rock in her hands again and felt its smooth contours. "Envy followed the little girl like a homeless dog." The old woman's eyes were distant.

" . . . Envy?"

"Yes, Doctor, envy. The other children of the village shunned the special one, because this little girl knew of a restful, beautiful place that the others did not know. No death, no fighting, no disease, no hunger, no greed—no soldiers coming in the night."

Harvey looked out the window again, noticing the strong wind jostling the branches of a eucalyptus tree.

"Where is this place?"

"A place within her own mind, Dr. Black. But, perhaps more than that . . ."

Harvey's eyes moved to the teacher's, locking onto the wrinkled crevices of radiant intelligence. "Is this what you wanted to talk to me about?"

"Not entirely, Doctor. Your daughter is quite beautiful."

The teacher put down the stone and picked up the painting again, then handed it to Harvey. "But, the village children in my old country were not just jealous. They were also *afraid*."

"Afraid?"

He took the offered painting in his hands, examining the black and narrow box.

"Yes. You see—fear, and then *death*—followed the little girl too."

Harvey put down the painting. He rose slowly from his chair. "I wonder why Rebecca painted her black clothes chest. She has one just like that in her bedroom."

Pearl stood up too, teetering a bit over her chair. "That's not what she told me."

"What are you talking about?"

The teacher pointed to the little black ovals on the sides of the rectangular object on the painting.

"See these dots on the box, Doctor?"

Harvey glanced at them.

"Yes, so?"

"These are handles for *carrying, not opening*, Dr. Black."

Pearl slowly hobbled around her desk to position herself in front of Rebecca's father—up close, her eyes fastened to his.

"It is not a clothes chest, Doctor."

Harvey stepped back slightly.

"What is it then?"

"You see—," her eyes took on strangeness, "—it is not a clothes chest, it is rather . . . a *coffin*."

"Now, Mrs. Johnson, we have many options—your cancer may *remit* too."

Rachael explained to the sobbing young black woman sitting gowned upon the exam table. "We have the chemotherapy, then there's radiotherapy and also a new drug on the market—then *surgery* . . ."

At the mention of "surgery," the patient grabbed Rachael's hand.

Rachael sat on the stool beside her patient, reflexively removing her hand from the clutches of her distraught patient. She then scooted her stool away from her slightly.

"I mean, Mrs. Johnson, surgery is only an *option*. But, the situation could be worse. Stage two breast cancer is better than stage three, isn't it?"

I hate this, thought Rachael. *What is wrong with this patient?* Doesn't she understand when something *good* happens! It could be much worse.

I'm sick of all this drama in my life, lamented Rachael.

Mrs. Johnson looked around the sterile, battleship-grey room with hanging pictures of cancer survivors smiling broadly into the camera— marketing testimonials that didn't quite match the desperate expression upon her face.

"My *God*, Dr. Black—*please*—I'm so scared! What can I do?"

There's noting else, thought Rachael. *Don't you understand?*

Listen lady, I just told you what you can do!

Rachael got to her feet to attend to the paperwork resting on the counter. "Of course you're scared . . ."

Rachael cracked a pat smile and continued shuffling her papers as she ran though her list of reassuring clichés. She then wrapped up the appointment pronto. " . . . I'm sure you'll do well."

"But Doctor—"

"—Return in thirty days. Here's your lab work. Have a nice day, Mrs. Johnson." Rachael marched into her deserted office, slamming the door behind her.

She growled at herself.

"*Have a nice day!*"

I can't believe I said that!

She plopped down on the padded oak chair behind her antique, roll-up desk and closed her eyes, her hands shaking. "I hate this goddam job!"

Letting out a sigh, she yanked open the drawer and pulled out a piece of paper with an envelope attached to it. She ripped off the envelope, throwing both papers down on the desk.

Grabbing a pen, she mouthed under her breath the words of resignation—a work in progress—as she scribbled on the paper: " . . . '*Dear Red Shield, I am terminating my employment as of* . . .'"

A knock at her door and it swung wide open. A fat nurse with too much lipstick bellowed into the room from the entrance, her pudgy hands resting upon her broad hips, "The next one's here, Doctor, she needs a radical too."

Rachael glared at the nurse.

"Please remember to refer *this time* to a Red Shield surgical facility. Are we good with that, Doctor Black?"

Rachael threw her papers into the drawer and sprung out of her chair. She rushed out of the room, passing the nurse at the door like two freight trains speeding in opposite directions.

"I ate something bad, I need a minute," Rachael fibbed.

The distraught physician rushed down the hallway and into the empty lavatory, locking the door behind her. Rachael rushed to the stall, throwing open the door and plopping down upon the commode.

She buried her head in her hands as she sobbed, desperately trying to mute the pitiful sound of her desperate cries.

"I hate . . . this goddam job!"

"Time to eat, Rebecca!" Harvey called out to his daughter from the patio door, as she swam in the pool, diving and splashing. "We're having Sunday breakfast!"

He saw more yellow leaves on the old maple tree as he looked out onto the pool, taking note of the slight nip in the early morning air.

"Take off your suit. Put on your thick cotton robe. It's getting cold out there."

Harvey sat at the kitchen table, which was loaded with hotcakes, real maple syrup, soft butter in a big tub, and a bowl of fresh blueberries from the local farmer's market.

Rebecca joined him in her white robe with the Hello Kitty patches sewn into the sleeves.

"Where's Mother?" His daughter had brought to the table a small painting placing it face up next to the pitcher of milk.

Harvey passed her the hotcakes. "She's working. Do you want syrup?" He stuffed his mouth full of blueberries.

Rebecca nodded. "She works hard, doesn't she?"

"Yes, very hard—too hard." He handed her the syrup. "Is that painting from your school?"

"Yes, Father."

He recognized the familiar subject of the piece, what looked like the same maple tree that was in their back yard, only with bare branches.

It had a caption below it.

Harvey put down his fork. "Let me see it."

She handed him the painting.

Harvey glanced out the kitchen window to compare the maple by the pool with the picture. "It's our maple tree, isn't it?"

"Yes, Father." Rebecca piled blueberries on her plate.

Mindful that his daughter had always called him "father" and his wife "mother"—instead of the usual "mommy" and "daddy"—he thought it was yet another one of Rebecca's quirks, even suggestive of a bygone era. He found this endearing, although a bit strange.

"What's this writing below your painting? Let's see," Harvey read it out loud, "'All *Together.'*"

He didn't quite know what to make of the words, but let it pass.

"Do you like it?" Rebecca poured the syrup over her blueberries.

"Yes. About Thanksgiving time, the maple will be bare, and then you can paint it again from real life."

Rebecca looked out the window at the tree. "That will be a special time for all of us."

Harvey rose from the table, walked over to the drawer next to the refrigerator, taking out a spool of tape. He then walked over next to the window and taped the painting to the kitchen wall.

"There!" He smiled at Rebecca. "Let's have more pretty paintings."

A dark memory then shot into his head—the painting of the long, black box that Pearl Nguyen had shown him—the coffin.

He decided to say nothing about it.

"All right," said Rebecca as she stared out the window absently, "more paintings. Study them very closely, Father."

Rachael cleaned off the deep shelves in the master bedroom, walk-in closet. She picked up the dirty laundry from the white carpet, when she noticed a glittering object next to a red bathing suit. It rested on the second shelf.

She bent over, taking it in her hands.

"Rebecca's wet goggles again," she moaned under her breath. "The wet swimsuit too!"

She marched out of the master bedroom closet and over to Rebecca's closed bedroom door down the hall, the soggy swim suit in her hand, ready to punish her daughter for leaving her wet things in her closet again.

Pushing the child's door open wider, she saw that the room was empty.

Rachael, dressed in her black gym shorts and a grey-cotton tank top, and then made a beeline to Rebecca's bathroom down the hall, noticing the chink of light below the closed door. She heard her daughter splashing in the bathtub.

Rebecca's muffled voice filtered through the door. The child was conversing with herself again, she thought.

Rolling her eyes in disgust, Rachael put her ear close to the door, just making out the little girl's next sentence:

"We're going away soon, aren't we Water Lady? Then we'll all be together. It's so beautiful and peaceful there—not like here."

Rachael threw down the swimsuit and banged hard on the door. No answer—she did it again, and still no answer.

She turned the knob—locked.

Then, the door opened a crack.

Rachael saw her daughter standing at the door—dripping wet—with a large, pretty, green stone in her hand. The surprised mother pushed the door wide open and barged in, grabbing a pink towel from the rack.

"Make yourself decent!" She threw the towel at her daughter. "What's that in your hand?"

Rebecca backed up from her mother. "A present from the Water Lady."

"Don't give me any more of this 'Water Lady' crap! Where did you get it?"

Rebecca, clutching the stone with one hand, draped the long towel over her wet body with the other, as she turned in an effort to keep the stone from her inquisitive mother.

"Give it to me!" screamed Rachael.

"It's mine!"

"Hand it over, now, young lady."

"No!"

"All right, no more pool."

Rebecca slowly obeyed, warily moving closer to her mother as she handed her the pretty object.

"Don't take it from me, please Mother."

Rachael's eyes widened as she examined the large, beautiful, aquamarine stone in her shaking hand.

"My goodness, where did you find this?"

Rebecca cried, "I told you."

She tried to snatch it back from her mother's strong hands, but missed as Rachael pulled it away.

"*She* gave it to me."

"Get dressed! You're grounded, Rebecca. No TV, no trips with your friends, no shopping, no allowance, not even dinner tonight!"

"Please give me back the stone. The Water Lady gave it to me."

"THERE IS NO WATER LADY!"

Rebecca threw off her towel and plopped back into the tub, submerging herself chest deep in the water. As her mother continued to scream, the little covered her ears.

Dr. Harvey Black, standing in front of a big screen, lectured to the medical residents seated in the dark auditorium. He pointed with his lazar-pointer to a pathological mass on the slide-projected image of a liver.

"You'll probably see the clinical manifestations of this malignancy in your patient rounds. Look for increased bleeding tendencies, easy bruising, and weight loss. I read films . . ."

Harvey—all of a sudden—mysteriously threw the pointer down on the podium next to him and bolted out the side door. The students looked on, then at each other, with astonishment . . .

His yellow VW screeched to a halt in his home driveway next to Rachael's parked, red Lexus. He jumped out of his car, dashing around the side yard and past the gate to the pool deck in the back yard.

He saw Rebecca lying on the tiles below the huge maple tree.

The little girl held her ankle as she writhed in agony. Noticing her father sprinting towards her in his long, white lab coat, she reassured him, "I'm all right. I just fell."

Harvey crouched beside her to examine her ankle. "What happened? I *knew* something was wrong. I *felt* it!"

"I was waiting for mother to take me to school. Then I climbed the tree to get a pretty leaf, and I fell." She pointed to her leg. "It hurts when I walk."

Dr. Black looked her over carefully, satisfied that she had just suffered an ankle strain and nothing more serious. "How high did you climb?" He glanced up at the tall maple overhead.

Rebecca rubbed her ankle. "Near the top."

"Rebecca! You know better." He looked over to the back of the house. "Where's your mother?"

"She's riding her exercise bike in the spare room. She couldn't hear me yell for help."

Rachael dashed into the back yard as Harvey helped Rebecca to her feet, the child sporting a slight limp.

"What on earth happened?" she screamed, putting her arm around her daughter with an earphone hanging around her neck. Her black nylon shorts and shirt dripped with sweat as she released Rebecca from her embrace.

"She fell out of the tree," said Harvey. "I think she's OK."

"What were you doing up there?" Rachael composed herself, fear quickly giving way to anger. "Tell me, Rebecca!"

"I was picking a beautiful leaf."

"Is this the leaf, honey?" asked Harvey as he spotted it lying on the ground. He picked it up.

"Yes, that's it."

It was yellow with a lot of fire-red, more colorful than the other yellow leaves lying on the deck.

"It *is* beautiful." Harvey handed it to his wife.

"Why would you do something so dangerous and stupid, Rebecca?" Rachael threw the leaf to the ground.

The little girl looked at the pool. "To give it to *her*."

"I thought so!"

Rachael then eye-punched Harvey. "What are you doing home, Harvey?"

"I sensed that she was hurt. So . . ."

"You *sensed* she was hurt! *So*, I now have *two* psychos on my hands. I don't believe it."

"I just had this premonition—"

"—No more swimming, Rebecca," screamed Rachael.

"Now, that's not necessary, is it Rachael?" pleaded the father. "She loves it so, and it's her only exercise."

"Shut up, Harvey. I'm through being understanding. Why don't you get back to work?"

There was a long silence as all three stood there, glaring at each other.

Then, Rachael's lip started to quiver.

"What's wrong, Rachael?" asked Harvey softly.

"You've stopped helping—to pull the wagon, Harvey," she answered, "that's what's wrong!" She threw up her hands. "I need help too," she yelled. "I'm tired!"

"Rachael—"

"I hate you!" screamed the mother at her husband.

Rebecca slowly backed away from them, shaking her head. She put her hands over her ears.

"Stop it!"

She limped toward the house, then turned back to glare at her parents.

"We're not *together*."

Dr. Carmen Navarro, MD, sat behind her desk with her hands in a tight fist, one squeezing the life out of a pen. She wore all black, as if in perpetual mourning.

Her shiny, black hair wound in a tight bun, like her fists. The heavily lidded eyes—also black— were faintly visible behind the large, steel-rimmed eyeglasses that had a grey tint in the lenses. Her only trace of color was her loud, red lipstick, painted in two thin stripes, which seemed to part with great effort as she spoke.

"Rebecca's condition is very serious, I'm afraid. I'll see her in a moment. I wanted to see you two first."

The psychiatrist spoke to Harvey and Rachael from far across her huge desk as her eyes roamed furtively and restlessly behind the lenses.

"The child is very intelligent, with an IQ of one-sixty. To her, abstractions are as real as objects. The Water Lady under the pool drain represents a life force, a powerful being, a *protector*, of sorts."

"Protector from what?" asked Harvey.

"Why, from herself, of course."

"From herself?" Rachael shifted in her chair, and then leaned forward. "Can you explain that?"

"This is a very dangerous condition. I've been seeing her for a month now, but there's no improvement—even with medication. The coffin in the picture represents a kind of death wish," explained Navarro.

The psychiatrist smiled inappropriately.

"The fall from the maple tree, submerging to the pool drain, the dark, leafless tree painting—they symbolize obsession with death . . ."

"Do you mean she's *suicidal*, Dr. Navarro?" Harvey asked. "Or, does she only want to escape her troubles somehow?"

"Good question." Navarro leaned back in her chair and pursed her lips. "Either way, volitional acts directed by the subconscious could result in great physical harm."

Navarro gestured with an open hand to Rachael. "We must avoid a—" she glanced over at the photograph resting upon the bookshelf of a young, dark-haired, rather melancholy-looking boy—"a *tragedy*."

She continued in a less brassy tone, looking down at the floor. "A tragedy like the one that befell my little boy last year. A result of a similar fantasy that must be . . . *expunged*."

Harvey and Rachael looked over at the photo, and then each other. Rachael nodded gently, her voice sympathetic. "You mean *hospitalize* Rebecca, don't you Carmen? Is Rebecca really that sick?"

Harvey: "No!" Navarro: "Yes!"

Both persons quickly answered Rachael's question simultaneously, but in heated opposites.

Navarro scowled at Harvey. "Yes," she repeated, with a note of triumph.

"She doesn't seem that bad, Dr. Navarro," blurted Harvey plaintively.

"As they say, '*Things are not always as they seem*'," Navarro responded coolly. "Just a short inpatient stay—that's what Rebecca needs."

"We could move, or take out the pool," offered Harvey as he looked at his wife for support.

Dr. Navarro nodded as if explaining a math problem to a slow pupil, "Now, Harvey, that would just be putting a bandage on a deep, underlying wound, wouldn't it? Next time, it would be something else."

Harvey stood up to leave the room as he rolled his eyes at the pat clichés. "All right, Dr. Navarro, we'll think about it. Let's go, Rachael."

He headed for the door. "It's time for Dr. Navarro to see Rebecca," he added in a doubtful voice.

Harvey and Rachael left the room as Navarro's cautious eyes followed them . . .

Presently, Dr. Navarro's nurse brought in Rebecca, dressed in a bright, pink dress. The little girl sat down on the tan couch opposite the desk as the psychiatrist signaled for the nurse to leave.

The door slammed shut.

The psychiatrist stared at Rebecca, her steely gaze sizing up her pretty patient. "Now, Becky . . ."

"My name's *Rebecca*."

"*Rebecc*a, it may be that you'll be visiting us in the hospital soon." Navarro cracked another tight smile, "your parents and I are discussing it."

"No, I won't—"

"—We may try a stronger medicine, too," rejoined Navarro quickly as she talked over the child, "what do you think of that?"

"I won't!"

Dr. Navarro looked over at the photograph on the bookshelf, and then opened her notebook. She wrote something down, shaking her head. "We shall see."

"No!"

The doctor frowned. She took off her glasses, her eyes becoming cinders burning brightly. The red line of her painted lips became two, the tight smile forced.

"Look, you're here to straighten out your self-destructive behavior. I'm here to see that you do. Now, where did we leave off last time? Oh yes, you've been a headstrong little girl as far as you can remember, haven't you?"

She wiped her glasses off and put them back on. "We'll have to fix that."

Harvey and Rebecca sat in front of the DVD player together on the big, leather couch in the den, sipping on sodas and eating chips. They watched *Old Yeller*, the Disney classic movie about the loyal dog and the struggling pioneer family. As the picture ended, both sat with misty eyes.

Harvey stroked his daughter's hair and asked, "How's it going with Navarro?"

"She doesn't understand," said Rebecca.

"Understand what?"

"That I'm going away for a long visit soon, to a place that's far more beautiful and nice."

"You mean under the pool drain, with the Water Lady?"

"Yes, the drain is her window to a wonderful world of new shapes and colors—and sounds too— soothing sounds you've never heard before. I want you and mother to come with me. We'll leave though the window—to be *free*—before it's too late!"

"Too late?"

"Yes, the window will close, and I'll never come back again."

A tear rolled down Rebecca's cheek. "I don't want to leave you!"

Harvey slumped in the couch, dropping his head in his hands.

"What's wrong?" she asked.

"I've got something to tell you, darling."

"What?"

"I've decided."

"Decided what?"

"Just now."

Harvey raised his head out of his hands and looked his daughter square in the eye.

"I'm closing the pool soon."

"Please, no!" Rebecca grabbed his arm, pleading. "When?"

"Soon. That's . . . not all, honey. It's *my* decision too. Tomorrow, your mother and I are taking you to the hospital—to Dr. Navarro—for a short stay—"

"—No!" screamed Rebecca, jumping up from the couch."

She ran out of the den and into her bedroom, slamming the door.

"You can't! I won't let you."

Harvey closed his eyes.

He could hear her sobbing in her room all the way from the den.

Again, he buried his head in his hands.

Dr. Black had tossed and turned all night, listening to the strong wind jostling the leaves of the yellow-leafed maple tree. Rachael was sound asleep next to him.

The sun's orange rays were just becoming visible on the horizon. As the birds chirped strongly outside the bedroom window, Harvey threw his robe on over his pajamas. He crept past the door and down the hall, making his way to the patio.

He thought he had heard something outside not five minutes before, perhaps the wind jostling the waves in the pool or a bird landing in water.

As he arrived at the pool, he could smell the scent of the chlorine mixed with the jasmine. He then noticed that the wind had blown some laundry in the pool and it had gone to the drain . . .

Later, it was said that the neighbors could hear Harvey's screams from the next block.

The rest of the morning's memories and images collided with one another. There was the cold plunge in the pool and the wicked sound of voices sobbing, choking, screaming, and groaning.

There were the medics and police.

He had huddled over his daughter's drowned body.

It lay stiff and motionless upon the Mexican tile deck, with a blanket over the head.

For, he had found Rebecca at the drain, his little daughter as lifeless as one of her pretty stones.

Part Two:

The cold rain drenched the black, child-sized casket. Several dozen mourners, dressed heavily in black with umbrellas on the unseasonably cold morning, huddled with the pastor as she intoned the last rites at the gravesite, her soothing voice mixing with the suppressed cries and whispers.

Harvey and Rachael stood next to the coffin—it eerily resembling Rebecca's painting—as three men and a woman carefully lowered it into the earth beside the gravestone.

When the ritual was completed, Harvey took Rachael's arm and left the site, only to be greeted by a dark, stooped, and veiled figure holding a small box. The old woman silently offered the box to Harvey, her yellow teeth visible through the withered lips.

"For you, Dr. Black," she whispered, pushing the box in his hands, "Rebecca painted this one too, in my classroom."

The old woman was Pearl Nguyen.

Harvey took the box. "I refuse to believe she's gone," his scratchy voice cracking with grief, "do you hear me? Could it be that she's still with us—*somewhere*—in some form, Pearl?"

She looked at Mrs. Black carefully, and then at Harvey, nodding.

"Perhaps that is true."

She then hobbled off in the rain. "Perhaps it is true."

Rachael shook her head angrily, pulling Harvey with her as she made a quick exit toward the parked car. "Who invited *her*?"

"I did."

"What did she give you?"

Harvey looked down at the object in his hands.

"Hope."

The sweet little hand pointed upward, with two big hands reaching down toward it. The one big hand was smooth with tapered fingers and lavender-painted nails, and the other a man's hand, with a thick, gold wedding band adorning the fourth finger.

The background in the painting—solid blue-green—clashed with the yellow kitchen wallpaper as Harvey taped Rebecca's latest painting to the wall, next to her painting of the bare maple tree.

"We'll see her again," said Harvey with conviction. He sat down at the kitchen table with a tear in his eye. Rachael strode into the room with a stack of plates, setting the table for a late supper.

"*I said*, we'll see her again," he added.

Rachael put down the plates and took a seat next to her husband. She gently placed her hands upon his shoulders, her eyes searching his. "She's gone, Harvey."

He shook his head.

She looked at the paintings. "It's no use keeping those around. But, if it makes you feel better—"

"—Rebecca's *not* gone. I feel it. Remember the time I rushed home from work when she fell out of the tree? I felt *that* too—."

"—Listen to me—"

"—She wants us with her—see the painting?" He pointed to the wall. "She's reaching out to us."

His wife paused, letting out a deep breath. "Dinner's ready soon."

"I'm not hungry."

Rachael stood up, shaking her head in silence, leaving the room to complete a few other chores before the meal. She headed down the hallway, her stride quickening with each step.

She picked up the large laundry basket at the utility alcove and marched into her master bedroom closet. Picking Rebecca's red bathing suit and glitter-rimmed goggles out of the basket, she placed them gently upon the middle shelf.

Rachael studied the objects closely and then closed her eyes, feeling their textures.

Overcome with grief, she slammed the closet door shut, and then plopped down on the floor of the closet below the shelf.

She screamed for her dead little daughter as loud as she could, but no one answered.

The tall, black police officer standing at the reception desk eyed the dapper, middle-aged man as he approached the thinning, brown hair and the thoughtful but subdued, brown eyes suggesting a gentle nature.

"Officer, I live close by on Birch Street," the demure man explained in a soft tone, "my name is Harvey Black. I called about those rocks that I found in the canyon—the ones I picked up in the bushes in back of my home."

The grey-haired policeman smiled and held out his large hand. "Oh yes, I'm Sargent Wilson, Jim Wilson." They shook hands. Wilson noted the sadness in the man's eyes. Recalling the name of the visitor, he realized the reason behind the sadness.

"I checked our database, Dr. Black, and it came up blank."

"Then, there's no record of any local burglaries or thefts involving semi-precious stones, such as aquamarine or onyx or opals, and the like?"

"None."

"No such contraband has been found in the canyons nearby, or in vacant fields or in the parks?"

"No sir. Looks like you have finders-keepers. Why such an interest in these stones, sir, if you don't mind my asking?"

"Nothing, officer, my little girl just has a strange imagination, that's all. Thanks for your help."

"My pleasure, sir." Wilson watched Harvey intently as he left the station . . .

As he drove to work for the first time after a week's absence, he thought about the stones that Rebecca had claimed were given to her by the Water Lady. How on earth did she really get them? One she had claimed at least—the large opal—was worth real money.

Where could Rebecca have found it? What about the others? Then, he started to think about Pearl Nguyen's strange, brown rock that sat on her desk— the one that gave off heat.

Weird . . .

He remembered Pearl's bizarre story of the "special" little girl from her village back in Vietnam. This little girl also knew of a "restful, beautiful place," just as his daughter had described.

As Harvey drove on the highway, the heavy fog and tail lights of the cars in front of him danced with the corners of his mind as the car engine droned, lulling him into a sense of void.

Could such places be real? Certainly not—he was a medical scientist, not a sorcerer.

However, Harvey recalled one incident long ago, when he was a very young man.

He had stood directly behind a young girl who was picking flowers in a field. He had been maybe a hundred yards from her. Not making a sound, he just stared at the back of the girl's head, admiring the beauty of the color of her hair. It had matched the color of the flowers almost exactly.

All of a sudden, the girl had turned around and looked back at him!

How did she know he was staring at her?

Harvey, a scientist, knew that it was impossible to explain *rationally*—there was simply no *physical* explanation, none whatsoever. Could it have been just coincidence? Or instinct?

No, he thought not . . .

It was something beyond the senses and beyond reason, he had decided.

Presently, he arrived at his clinic . . .

"Dr. Milford, I need a month off."

Milford's jaw dropped just a bit. "Harvey, as I've said so many times, we're all simply *devastated* by your recent bereavement—my *gosh*." Milford, rolling his eyes, leaned back in the chair behind his huge desk as Harvey sat across it, "*but . . .*"

Harvey didn't listen to the details, but did hear the inevitable "you advance or you go" near the end of the speech, only repeated in softer tones than usual.

"Tell you what, Harvey, you can do what you want, but I suggest—for your own good—for you to take two weeks off instead, and then let's talk."

"All right, Dr. Milford, two weeks it is."

Whisk—out the door, *adios*, goodbye, and no more Milford or the clinic for a while, anyway.

Harvey thought things over.

Rebecca can't be gone. It's impossible. Things like this just don't happen.

They don't happen to me, anyway.

"I had to see you, I knew you'd understand." Harvey stood at the blackboard with Pearl Nguyen as she posted the next assignment for the class, which was out on lunch recess.

"You don't believe it either— that my daughter's really gone. Well, do you Pearl?"

Pearl looked at Harvey with heavy eyes, and then continued writing with her chalk. "I wonder too. She had a strong force." The teacher then coughed heavily.

"Tell me more about the little girl in your village back in Vietnam."

Harvey looked up at the string of white letters on the blackboard. The basic math lesson brought back distant memories of his grade school back in Cape Elizabeth, Maine.

"What happened to the strange child?"

Pearl's hand started to shake as she wrote on the board. "One day, she disappeared into the sea— but, not quite."

"Water again."

"Yes, into the sea. She left behind—I'm not sure of the word in English—can we say, '*beacons*'?"

"What?"

Pearl stopped writing the arithmetic symbols and drew a round figure with stripes and crosshatches. "This is . . . what I *feel*. I think of Rebecca, and I *sense* this symbol."

Harvey studied the drawing, which looked like a special rock of some kind. "What's that?"

Pearl shrugged. "It is what I feel."

She put down the chalk and hobbled to her desk as Harvey followed. "You are from Maine, are you not, Doctor? Are there . . . lighthouses there?"

"Lighthouses—why, yes."

Harvey stood in front of her desk, eyeing the strange, brown stone lying on top. "How did you know where I'm from?"

Pearl sat down behind her desk and stared at the brown stone.

"Little Rebecca told me."

"Oh yes, of course."

Pearl breathed heavily.

"Then, you know what a lighthouse *does*." She slowly picked the rock up off the table and offered it to him.

"If Rebecca is still with us, she will tell you, Doctor. She will leave . . . *beacons*. They will show you the way, like a lighthouse. Think of your home— think of *where she likes to be*, and you may find her."

Harvey, standing over the diminutive teacher, slowly took the warm object in his hand, feeling again its strange energy.

"The little girl in my village—the one who disappeared into the sea—was a very beautiful child."

The school children returned from lunch.

"Water and earth stones are but two sides of the same thing," the old woman added.

Harvey put the brown stone back on her desk. "I'll go now, Pearl. But first, did the little girl back in Vietnam leave you any *specific* signs? Were there any clues that she was still with you—any *beacons*?"

"Your daughter will show you if she is still with you. Do no despair, Dr. Black." Pearl coughed again.

"Please tell me—I must know. What did she leave behind?"

Pearl's eyes moved to the laughing children entering the classroom, ready to resume her class.

Then, they shifted to the brown stone.

She smiled.

"You just had it in your hand, Doctor."

Harvey reclined in the green-leather chair, listening to Dr. Carmen Navarro explain that his depression, and that his "unhealthy obsession," is due to his denial of Rebecca's fate. Looking up at the high, angular ceiling in the dimly lit psychiatric office, he wondered how many adult patients Carmen had treated in the same, soft chair that he sat in.

"Your wife has accepted your child's death, Harvey." Dr. Navarro sat on the couch opposite him, her steely dark eyes—obscured by her steel-rimmed eyeglasses—roving the numerous rows of books lining her shelves. "Rachael's put it past her and has moved on. Eventually, you will too."

Harvey closed his eyes, his mind filling in the unspoken remainder of her comment: " . . . And *you* should be back to work too, Harvey."

For once, he felt the anger build inside him, and the desire to express it—so he did. "Rebecca told me before she . . . left us, that you didn't understand her, Dr. Navarro."

Navarro's head jerked in her patient's direction, not used to such push back.

"We know that little Rebecca was a very sick child, now don't we?" Her fist grew tighter as she squeezed the pen in her hand. "Look at what happened."

Harvey's eyes flashed at her. "She is a loving child—a very gifted child," he shifted his weight forward in his chair, "how much did she tell you about the Water Lady?"

"'*Is*?'" You said '*is*' Dr. Black. Rebecca's been dead for many weeks."

Navarro's tight smile crept up from the crevices of her mind, as if she scored a dark triumph. "Your daughter, as sweet as she was, definitely had an underside to her."

"Underside? What are you talking about?"

"Your anger is healthy, Dr. Black."

"Screw my anger! What did she tell you?"

Navarro's gaze burned into her patient. "Becky told me that she was going away, and that she wanted to take you and Rachael with her. If we stopped her, then life wouldn't be worth living. Of course, she was talking metaphorically . . ."

Harvey shot up from his chair. He shook with rage. "'*Metaphorically*' my ass! We found her at the bottom of the damn pool! Why didn't you tell us?"

Navarro, nodding in a cool and self-assured manner, put down her notebook and removed her glasses, revealing eyes completely devoid of emotion. "Remember, Dr. Black, that *I'm* the one who wanted to hospitalize her, long before you had consented."

Harvey bolted out of the room, slamming the door behind him. Dr. Navarro's smile faded as she watched him go. She looked up at the photo of her departed son.

Rachael came home from work, her hair mussed, her voice muted, her quick step checked. The lights were on and Harvey's car rested in the garage, but she noticed that the house was completely quiet.

She opened the fridge door to survey what to eat, and then slammed it shut—her appetite having left her. Rachael walked down the hallway past the open master bedroom door and peeked in, her husband not in sight.

Then she glanced down the dim hall to Rebecca's closed bedroom door, and sensed he was in there . . .

"What are you doing in here?"

Rachael saw her husband sit up as she opened the door, his excited eyes catching hers. There he lay, in his brown pajamas, over Rebecca's covers, the small reading lamp throwing off a soft yellow light.

"What's that in your hand, Harvey?"

Harvey held up a piece of paper. "It's something I found between the mattress and the box-spring. I turned over in the bed and heard this rustling—"

"—Why is the window open?" Rachael folded her arms. "This room is cold."

"The wind is an earth element, you know," blurted Harvey.

"I see." Rachael's face froze, her eyes wide. "Of course it is."

The chilling wind blew in from the open window near the bed. Rachael saw the branches of the huge maple that was lit up from the motion-detecting patio lights. The branches shifted in the wind, the leaves a billow of bright red.

"I'm tired Harvey, what are you doing in here?"

"You *look* tired, Rachael."

She looked at the picture Harvey held up from the bedspread.

"See Rachael, another painting. It's Rebecca's." He pointed to the black circle with the crosshatches.

"I've seen this pattern before—last week, in Pearl Nguyen's classroom. She predicted it, so to speak"

Rachael slowly approached Harvey, her lips quivering.

"What were you doing in Rebecca's old classroom?"

"Learning things. I've been back there a couple of times, too." He put the painting down and got up from the bed, approaching Rachael slowly as she stood there in the middle of the room, staring at her husband in disbelief.

"There are things, I always felt, but didn't really know. Pearl explained them."

She backed up from him. "I don't want to hear it. You're not feeling well."

Harvey held out his hand. "Come with me next time. We can visit Pearl."

"I'm going to bed." Rachael backed up more, her eyes not leaving his, shaking her head. "I had a hard day."

She turned and quickly left the room.

Harvey's eyes followed her closely as she left, and then he made for the kitchen with Rebecca's painting in hand.

He took the tape out of the drawer and taped Rebecca's third painting up to the wall, next to her other two: the picture of the bare-leafed maple; and the picture of the small hand reaching up to the two other adult hands. Now, this one of the round, crosshatched and stripped object was there too.

Harvey looked down at the caption under the painting of the bare maple tree, reading again to himself the words that his departed daughter had written before she died.

"'ALL TOGETHER.'"

"He's going off the deep end. I know he is." Rachael sat on the couch across the office from Dr. Carmen Navarro, who sat at her desk, assiduously taking notes.

The light from the window made the pert psychiatrist's photo-grey glasses even darker, the sun's rays reflecting off her eyeglasses, "Let's see, Rachael, my journal entries tell me that your husband is having trouble at work, is he not?"

"Yes, the Medical Director—I think—sees my husband as a dilettante. Maybe worse . . ."

"You mean, *unstable*?"

Navarro glanced over at Rachael, nodding energetically, apparently content with the progress of her enquiries. "This goes along with his history of magical thinking and his susceptibility to obsessive behavior—such as his focus on poor little Becky. The incident in her bedroom is concerning."

"*Becky*?"

"Rebecca, dear. Your departed daughter."

"Oh yes, of course."

Rachael shifted her weight on the couch and then cleared her throat. "I don't know what to do, Carmen—we need help. He signed the release about his personal health information—so you can explore anything you want with me."

Carmen's painted lips morphed into one red line as she squeezed her pen, her eyes narrowing. "Now, we can't have you *both* coming apart."

Rachael's quick eyes darted toward Navarro. "I haven't been sleeping well lately, I admit. Work is getting to me . . ."

Rachael shook her head and looked silently down at her lap, unable to continue.

"It's going to be all right," Carmen looked up at the picture of her dead little boy resting on the shelf. "Flight of ideas, obsessive-compulsive behavior, thought insertions, cravings to escape—this will stop. Your husband will get better. Will he come back in to see me?"

Rachael shrugged.

Carmen nodded to the photo, "If I had seen your husband sooner—perhaps with your daughter in group therapy—a tragedy may have been avoided. *My* personal tragedy with my son is another example. Early intervention is *critical*. Don't blame yourself, my dear."

Rachael frowned. "How do I handle my husband?"

"I'll tell you how. Don't indulge his fantasies. Be direct. Get him back to work as soon as possible! And, get him back in *here*."

"But—"

"—But nothing, it'll all pass—as it did with *you* last year.

Rachael glared at her doctor. "Well, yes—"

"—We both know that you have a psychiatric history, now don't we?" The red line became two as Navarro forced a smile. "You need your rest too, Rachael."

"We went over all that last year. You told me I was well—"

"—We don't want you to relapse just because your husband can't face facts, do we?"

"No, I suppose not."

Dr. Navarro stood up from her desk. "Fine. We're good here."

Rachael stood too. "I want to thank you Carmen, for everything."

The psychiatrist waved to the door, "You can tell Harvey I want to see him again soon." Carmen sat down at her desk. "I'll make time for him."

As Rachael walked to the door Carmen let out a sigh, "Rachael . . ."

She turned, "Yes Carmen?"

The psychiatrist said softly, "Your husband needs me desperately."

"Trick or treat!"

When Harvey opened the door Halloween night, his breath was sucked out of him.

Rebecca stood there on the porch holding the candy bag—right before his eyes!

His gaze drilled into the face of the little blonde girl costumed as a princess.

"Give me something good to eat!" she screamed.

Or, was it his little daughter after all?

The same height, the same build, the same assured tone of voice! A bead of sweat rolled down Harvey's cheek, smearing the clown makeup of his holiday costume.

He reached into the basket of Snickers candy bars and plopped one into her bag, leaning over to get a better look at the child.

He felt his plastic, bulbous clown-nose sipping off his real one, so he pushed it back in place.

"Well, well, who is under the princess mask?"

His heart raced as he gently pulled up on her mask just a bit to sneak a quick peek.

"Hey!" The fairy princess glared at Harvey, then looked over at her little brother—the devil. She laughed, and then glanced back at him, the strange clown standing over her at the door with his hand on her mask. "That's mine," she admonished.

Harvey let go, forcing a chuckle to smooth over his indiscretion. The little brown eyes under the silver mask didn't belong to Rebecca, and Harvey felt foolish, then sick. He smiled at the princess, and the little devil too and gently closed the door—then bolting it.

Harvey ran into the utility room and vomited his dinner into the sink, getting some on the washing machine standing next to it. Realizing that Rachael wouldn't want to come home to a smelly house, he took some cleaner and a rag from the cupboard and wiped down his mess.

As he crouched by the washer, he ran the rag over the bottom of it. He saw the harrowing object lying innocently upon the ground in the crack next to the sink.

What's happening to me, wondered Harvey?

Is this yet another red herring—like the little princess at the door?

Harvey threw down the rag and rubbed his eyes. He kicked the washer with his shin to send the pain up to his brainstem, making sure that he was indeed awake and alert.

It was there all right. It was no dream.

He picked up Rebecca's little pink sock and it was wringing wet, as though she had just thrown it there after a dip in the pool!

All of a sudden, an epiphany seized him.

He ran to the kitchen table with the wet sock and sat down on a chair, staring at Rebecca's paintings on the wall.

Rebecca hadn't really left us, Harvey exalted. He looked at the picture of the bare-leafed maple, and the caption below it. He then dashed out of the kitchen to the patio and to the maple tree.

The tree was bright red, with many of its leaves having already shed.

She's here!

The wet sock proves it! She'll be here until Thanksgiving, until the tree is bare—just three weeks more. Then, she's gone, and she wants us to go with her!

" 'All together' "

That's what the paintings are telling me!

Putting the sock to his face, he felt the soft, wet fabric. He smelled it, overjoyed to know that Rebecca's scent had lingered.

But, exactly where is she? How do I find her before she's gone for good?

Harvey entered the schoolyard around the time classes had let out for recess, walking into Pearl Nguyen's room after the children had left. To his astonishment, he didn't see the old Vietnamese woman that he had come to so admire, but rather a young and rather severe looking young woman at the blackboard.

She was slim and small chested, had very short, brown hair and nervous, electric-blue eyes. Wearing all khaki colors—including a coat and a thin tie that made her look very military—she held out her hand. Harvey took it.

"You're Dr. Black, aren't you?"

The firm grasp, short nails, and dry skin lent to her somber manner an especially austere undertone. "I'm Dana Maxwell, the substitute teacher."

"How did you know who I am?"

"Pearl . . . told me about you."

"*Told*, as in *past* tense?"

She hesitated.

"Where's Pearl? What happened to her?" Harvey had glanced down at the desk, noticing that her coveted brown stone was missing.

"There's something wrong, isn't there?"

"She's very sick. Things, well, don't look that good for her, frankly."

The cool blue eyes took on some mist as she spoke in a strange monotone that didn't quite match the context of her words.

"I don't have much time, in fact, you shouldn't even be here at all without checking in at the principal's office."

She hesitated, then walked behind the desk and opened the drawer anyway, taking out a small package. "Pearl's not only a colleague, but a very close . . . friend."

Standing across the desk, Harvey took the package as Dana handed it to him, her doubtful eyes taking in his shabby appearance.

His thin hair tussled, his face unshaven, and attired in a rumpled Polo shirt and wrinkled jeans--he looked as untidy as he felt.

"What's in the package?"

He then noticed the peculiar, silver amulet that hung around her neck, with a black-and-grey, crosshatched stone attached to it. The zebra-striped pattern was very familiar.

Dana slammed the drawer shut, her natural tension building. "I can only say she's on a plane back to her home country."

"Did she leave any word—?"

She pointed to the package. "—Just the book."

She moved briskly around the desk, picking her satchel up off the chair, ready to leave. "Pearl spoke highly of you, Doctor," her eyes shifted to the door, "I've told you all I know."

Harvey tossed and turned in his bed, hearing Rachael's heavy breathing as she lay asleep next to him, her little bottle of sleeping pills resting upon her nightstand. He rose from the bed, put on his robe, and walked out the bedroom and down the hall to his study—taking a seat behind his cherry wood desk.

He pulled open the drawer and gently placed the book in front of him, its faded, crimson cover facing him under the lamp.

Harvey read the odd title and subtitle under his breath": *Water and the Afterlife; Earth Stones and Life's Essence,*" by Yves Montmartre and P. Nguyen."

On the cover was a black, grey, and white symbol of a round object with crosshatches and crooked stripes, very similar to the zebra-pattern of his daughter's painting, the pattern on Dana's amulet, and Pearl's drawing on the blackboard.

"*Nguyen*," thought Harvey, "I wonder if it's any relation of Pearl's."

Probably not, that name is extremely common in Vietnam.

He turned to the front matter of the musty old tome.

"Translated into French and English and Vietnamese from the original Chinese edition; Copyright 1947, French Colonial Press, Saigon."

Harvey thumbed through the book as his breathing quickened. He read out loud from the brittle pages, which smelled of a strange combination of stale coffee and chai berry.

" . . . '*A spirit will revert to where it found harmony in life, and—in a chosen few—it is natural that it should be water. After all, most scientists will tell us that we originally came from water, even if that earth element was originally provided by a Great Creator.*'"

He turned to the middle of the book, to the black-and-white, picture insert. The caption at the top read, "Earth Stones."

There he saw simple photographs of many semi-precious stones, including opal, onyx, quartz, aquamarine, and, in the center, the large image of a "zebra onyx."

This was the same round, crosshatched, and striped stone that had become all too familiar.

A caption under it read: "Beacons to the Afterlife."

Harvey slammed the book shut. The notion hit him like a lightening bolt. *Find the zebra onyx, and I'll find Rebecca!*

He jumped up from his chair to commence his search . . .

Harvey turned his house upside down, searching every nook and cranny for the clue to his daughter's whereabouts. He knew that she was *somewhere*, but where?

Her bedroom did not aid his hunt again, nor did the kitchen—Rebecca's second most favored room.

There was no clue in the TV room, either. There were no more wet socks—and, to his great despair—no zebra onyx. He searched and searched, but nothing came up.

"Dr. Milford, I want more time off."

Harvey, in the time since his daughter's drowning, had become more self-assured and assertive.

He and Milford stood in line in the HMO cafeteria, which featured herring as their main entre.

Studying the baked fish resting in the serving bin, the Medical Director frowned. "Not bad, but not good either—I was hoping for meatloaf."

"Yes, meatloaf."

He glared at Harvey. "What did you say, Dr. Black?"

"—Meatloaf."

"No, before 'meatloaf'."

Harvey, dressed in his stained lab coat without a collared shirt or tie, slid his tray along the glass partition behind Milford, eyeing the food warily.

"I know you don't want to hear this," he took a tall glass of tea, glancing at his powerfully built boss, "I'm not ready to come back."

"You're right." Milford scowled at the cafeteria worker behind the glass, "Come on honey— put a few more fries on that plate!"

He turned his head sideways at Harvey, scanning his appearance over his eyeglasses, "I can *see* that. Why not?"

"I can't tell you."

"You *won't* tell me."

"I won't tell you."

"Do you remember what I said last time we talked?"

"Yes."

"What?"

"'I advance here or I go.'"

"All right then."

Milford stopped to ogle the custard and cherry pies, "I'm really glad to have you back, Harry."

"*Harvey*, sir, and I need more time."

"Did you tell the personnel office the same thing you told me?"

"Yes."

"Good."

Milford tightened his jaw as he grabbed a piece of pie, sliding his full tray along. Harvey followed.

"Dr. Black, you're not happy here."

"I'm not?"

"No. You don't want to work more hours. You don't wear a nice shirt and tie anymore. You don't like meatloaf."

"I need more time."

"You advance or you go."

"I know that."

There was a pause as Milford took out his wallet, standing in line to pay the cashier.

"Do you know what three day old fish is?"

"No sir."

"Huh?"

"I said no."

Milford's eyes darted around the room as they recognized key employees, nodding and smiling at them like a proud father at his son's little league baseball game.

"It's an unhappy doc in an HMO," he said, answering his own question. He snorted as he laughed.

"I'm not *un*happy, but—"

"—I know. Take all the time you want."

Milford then spun around and faced Harvey.

"In fact, Dr. Black, I'll accept your resignation today, effective in two weeks. You'll get two weeks off with pay."

Harvey started to speak. Milford put his hairy hand up. "Don't bother. You'll get references."

"I didn't—"

"—Otherwise—"

"—Yes, I know." Harvey nodded. "I advance or I go."

"Right!"

"I'm *gone*."

"Yes, you're gone."

He walked in the park and along the deserted beach, collecting his thoughts. Glancing over the vast, blue-green ocean and feeling the fresh, salty wind in his face, he focused his mind on Rebecca's posters, and other things too.

The crashing of the waves on the sand and the sound of the breezes gusting through the trees whispered to him. He sensed a new understanding of life and the energy that drives it. Something in his analysis of the situation was missing, though, and he didn't know what that was.

He had done a lot of thinking, and it was getting late and time to go home . . .

"I can do that, Rachael."

Harvey took one of the dirty dishes from the kitchen sink and washed it. His wife fussed with the rest of them, stuffing the already overloaded dishwasher.

She banged a dish as she threw the chipped plate into the machine. "They played Bach over the speaker at work today."

"You love Bach."

Rachael dropped a cup into the granite sink, breaking it. Harvey saw her hands shake.

"A nice change from the damn rockabilly crap that blares overhead night and day." Her voice cracked as she finished the sentence.

Harvey knew he was in for it.

"They play that stuff too at my . . . *work*." Harvey just realized that he hadn't given her the news yet about him getting fired at his work, so he had swallowed the word but not fast enough to ignite a row.

Rachael glared at him. "You were going to say your '*work*'? What *work*?" She slammed a drawer. "You were fired today!"

He put down the dishtowel. "Technically, I resigned."

Harvey tried to make light of it, but the savage eyes of his wife routed that impulse as she turned on him.

"Cute! Real cute—"

"—Good news travels fast," said Harvey.

"I have friends." She threw her towel down on the counter. "What do you think you are doing?"

Harvey started fooling with the dials on the dishwasher as he loaded it over capacity. She slapped his hand away from the dials.

"We don't talk anymore, Rachael."

She punched the heavy-load button.

"Whose fault is that?"

Harvey hesitated to tell her, and then decided to go ahead with it. "I've got something to show you."

He reached down into the bottom drawer and pulled out the old book that Pearl Nguyen had left him, *Water and the Afterlife*.

Rachael took the musty book in her hands, her eyes narrowing with skepticism.

"What the hell is this?" She flipped the pages as Harvey looked on.

"Pearl Nguyen gave me that book. She died yesterday. She knew Rebecca better than any of us."

Harvey turned the pages back to the cover.

"Oh she did, did she?"

"See the picture on the front—the zebra onyx?" Harvey pointed to Rebecca's painting on the far wall, "See Rebecca's painting on the wall—the last one? The zebra onyx—see how they match!"

Rachael nodded, her eyes blank but staring.

"See this—" Harvey bent over and removed Rebecca's pink bootie sock from the bottom drawer. "I found it—drenching wet—a couple of days ago next the washer."

"So?"

"Rebecca wore that *recently*—since she died. She used to swim in them, remember?"

He handed the sock to her. Rachael held the sock in one hand and the book in the other as if she had two skunks by their tails.

"I see," whispered Rachael absently.

"Look at Rebecca's other two paintings on the wall," Harvey pointed, "now look through the window to the maple tree!"

Rachael looked.

"Its leaves are red and almost bare." Harvey's voice cracked with emotion.

"She's with us. She's where the zebra onyx is hidden—here on our property!"

Rachael just stared at him.

"She wants us to be with her, in a better place. We only have a few days to find her—until the maple is bare—then she's gone forever!"

Rachael's eyes blazed. She threw the book at Harvey, missing him as he ducked, knocking the china off the nearby cabinet—it pieces smashing on the floor.

"You found a wet sock by the washer? How about ice in Alaska?" She threw the sock at him too.

Rachael rushed him, pushing him back hard.

"Do you mean to tell me that I slave away, day in and day out, in that horrible job of mine so you can indulge in fairly tales? What *are* you doing? You're nuts!"

"But—"

"—She's gone!"

"No—"

"—She'll never be back. *Never!*"

"Listen to me, please—"

Rachael grabbed him by his shirt collar.

"—You're not going to find her with some stupid stone!"

"Rachael, look at the pictures—"

"—You'll never find her *at all*. Get used to it!"

"Get used to it? Get used to *what*?"

Rachael shook Harvey by the collar and dragged him over to Rebecca's three paintings.

"It's called *life*! She's dead for Christ's sake!"

Rachael ripped the pictures off the wall and threw them down on the floor. "Don't you know what a wild imagination can do? These *damn* paintings! What damage it causes? *I* know."

She caught herself, her eyes welling up. "I learned when I was a girl. I learned when I saw my first psychiatrist. You must *control* yourself!"

Harvey tried to embrace her but she pushed him away. He slowly held out his hands to her. "What happened to you, Rachael? You've changed."

She shook her head.

Harvey put down his hands.

"What happened to your spirit?"

She just looked at him.

"What happened to your *imagination*?"

Her eyes burned into him.

"Your smile Rachael, when did you loose it?"

She sprung on him. She slapped him hard across the face.

"When did I lose it? I'll tell you. That's easy—I was in my lab coat. I lost it the first time that I sentenced a bright young patient to death with terminal cancer. They were guilty of nothing more than wanting to live!"

Harvey tried to take her in his arms but she pushed him away again, this time with a threating finger pointing at him.

"No one prepared me for that. And you're not even employed. Listen Harvey, and listen hard. You *are* going to see Dr. Navarro again this week—or we're done here—do you understand? You can pack your stuff and get the hell out!"

Harvey nodded slowly.

Rachael cupped her face in her hands and sobbed uncontrollably, then dashed out of the kitchen.

Harvey looked down at the floor. He picked up Rebecca's paintings off the ground and carefully put them in the bottom drawer.

As he slammed it shut, he swore to himself that he would find her.

We'll be together again, honey, I promise.

Part Three:

"So what are you now, a *spiritualist,* Dr. Black?"

Dr. Navarro peered at her patient over her opaque, steel-rimmed glasses as she sat at her desk, taking notes. "Rachael's very worried. She's also very tired. But, you shouldn't feel *quilt*."

Harvey sat on the couch, looking around at the frosty appearance of her office, then over at the photo of her deceased son on the bookshelf. He mused to himself that she mentioned the g-word precisely because that is what the doctor wanted him to feel.

"Why is that a nasty word, Dr. Navarro? *Spiritualism.* What about Abraham Lincoln, General George Patton, and Albert Einstein? They weren't exactly losers."

The thin, painted, parallel stripes came together, as her mouth contracted in scorn, "I'm surprised you haven't gone out and bought some scuba gear—and camped out at the drain in your pool," she said icily as she leaned forward in her chair, her voice having a sneering quality. "Your denial of your recent bereavement is unhealthy."

Harvey's epiphany jerked him up from the couch. "Of course! It's not the zebra onyx that's in Rebecca's painting, but the grid on the *pool drain!*"

"What did you say, Dr. Black? I didn't hear you."

"It was just a damn, stupid coincidence that the two things looked alike!"

He thumped himself on the head. "I'm so stupid. Like Pearl said, '*think where she likes to be,*'" shouted Harvey.

"I see," said Carmen with a quizzical expression.

Harvey dashed out of the office, leaving Navarro with an open mouth of puzzlement.

Rachael set the Thanksgiving table for their afternoon feast, which this year would include just her and Harvey. A store-bought turkey consumed in the kitchen and not the usual dining room would make the work easier, and wouldn't remind her as much of happier holidays past.

She glanced out the window at the maple tree which had completely shed its leaves, and the alarming spectacle of her husband—in full scuba gear and wetsuit—diving to the drain in their frigid pool.

She took her smart phone out of the pocket of her black sweats and touched the screen, " . . . Hello, Carmen, he's at it again! You said call any time. He's gone off the deep end, *literally* . . . He really thinks he'll find Rebecca down there in the pool drain . . . I'm worried now . . . What do we do? Is that necessary? I'll talk to him, but his *hospitalization* may be the only alternative—*soon* . . ."

Rachael put her phone away. She worried about Harvey. What if he gets worse, she wondered?

He may have to be admitted whether he wants to or not.

Looking out the window, Rachael saw him with that damn picture in his hand . . .

Harvey, outfitted in his diving gear, studied the image in Rebecca's painting carefully: a round, black figure with crosshatches and crooked stripes. He then looked up at the bare maple tree overhead, realizing that—it now being Thanksgiving—he had little time.

He thought of the words at the bottom of another picture.

"ALL TOGETHER."

He glanced down to the bottom of the pool to the blurred image of the black pool drain, its crosshatched, black, zebra-striped grid clearly visible despite the ripples within the water.

He looked between the painting and the pool drain. "That's it all right! She's in there somewhere, waiting for me!"

Carefully placing the painting down on the on the deck table, he fitted his mask, fins, and snorkel and then— abalone iron in hand—stepped down into the pool and dove to the drain.

As he pumped his fins and neared the drain, his heart pounded. Something—a bluish object—was in the drain!

Hovering over the drain, from the close angle he observed what looked like a large, blue stone caught on the inside of the grid—filling about a quarter of its round surface area.

Harvey jammed the iron into the crack around the grid and yanked it off, clutching the blue object in his hands. Pushing his other hand into the wide hole, he felt nothing else.

He saw no sign of Rebecca, the Water Lady, or a secret world beyond the drain—not yet!

He quickly resurfaced with the strange object after refitting the grid.

He removed his mask, snorkel, and fins, plopping down on the chair next to the table on the deck, surveying the wet discovery that he held in his hand.

It was a large, beautiful, turquoise stone. The Water Lady had placed it there for his little daughter.

How did it get there? How else? Is this not proof positive that the Water Lady—and Rebecca—are still with us?

He had been right all along, rejoiced Harvey.

He knew better than to tell his wife without more proof. So, he concocted a plan.

He took the pool manual off the table and studied it, careful to turn off the motor to the pool filter, so no more objects would be sucked down into the fourteen inch-diameter drain.

He dog-eared the page about the drain and threw it back on the table.

Next, he placed the blue stone back under the drain in the pool, seeing—from the surface—that it still filled about one fourth of the little squares under the surface area of the drain grid.

Now, he would monitor the drain from the deck almost every minute. The moment the blue stone disappeared, he would know his little Rebecca had taken it, so she would be nearby!

As extra bait, he expected something in a UPS shipment that morning. Dana Maxwell had called him and told him that she had shipped him two articles that Pearl Nguyen had left him in her estate. She had briefly described them to him.

Just then, Rachael, carrying a small package, entered the patio, stopping on the pool deck in front of Harvey. She eyed him warily.

"What are you doing, Harvey?"

"Fixing the pool drain—see the manual on the table?"

"Don't bullshit me." She threw the package on the deck table, "It's for you. They delivered it just a minute ago."

"How's the turkey and stuffing doing?"

"I want to talk to you about a short inpatient stay with Navarro."

There was a long silence.

Harvey stood up slowly and took Rachael's hand.

"Believe, Rachael. Get in touch with the child within you and forget Navarro."

He put his hands on her shoulders and drew her near to him, his voice intense. "Come with me! Come with *us*! Just believe me—please *believe*. Time is short."

Rachael's eyes gleamed for just a second, and then hardened with anger.

"You're nuts, Harvey. I'm getting you help whether you like it or not."

She stepped away from him and stormed out of the patio.

Harvey shook his head as he glanced at the package resting on the table. He ripped it open and took the two objects in his hands.

One was the beautiful, brown stone that had sat upon Pearl's desk. It felt warm in his grip. The other was his ultimate bait—his *insurance*.

He dove back down to the drain, and placed the second stone by the drain to ensure his daughter's reappearance: the beautiful, semi-precious earth stone—the prized zebra onyx . . .

Rachael ate Thanksgiving dinner alone at the kitchen table. She stared out the window at her husband, dressed in his bathing suit and windbreaker, keeping vigil under the patio lights by the pool. Its glow lent to Harvey's appearance a ghostlike aura.

A tear ran down her cheek as she dabbed at her turkey. She was dressed in her brown-and-yellow toned "holiday dress," sitting across from the table centerpiece—a grinning pilgrim . . .

Harvey looked into the lit pool and saw that the zebra onyx was still by the drain. He observed the turquoise stone through the drain grid, with no sign of his daughter.

He then noticed Rachael approaching him, aggressively striding with a forward lean—her jaws clenched. "I'm eating my Thanksgiving dinner all alone—" she bellowed at him.

"I'm waiting for Rebecca—"

Rachael froze in her tracks, stunned.

She glared down at him as he sat at the table, looking up at her contorted face. "I've had it, Harvey. I'm going to an attorney first thing next week."

"Rachael, you don't—"

"—I want a divorce." Her voice softened. "I'm sorry."

Harvey just sat, speechless and motionless.

Rachael marched back into the house before he could say a word.

Not altogether surprised, but wounded, he looked back toward the drain, and then off to the sight of the full moon visible over the bare maple tree. Despite renewed hope about his daughter, it had been a long, horrible day. He was dead tired, and getting drowsy.

He glanced back down at the drain.

The zebra onyx was gone!

He jumped to his feet, his eyes trained on the drain. The grid was still there, and he could see the blue color of the stone through the black metal grid.

But, it had changed! The blue stone now filled *half* the diameter of the drain—not a quarter.

Had the stone grown larger?

Next, he saw tiny bubbles floating up to the surface from the drain!

Harvey tore off his windbreaker and grabbed his mask and iron, plunging into the frigid water. He dove down to the drain.

There was still no sign of Rebecca.

Prying off the grid, he realized the stone was the same size, but what was it that had changed?

Then, it hit him.

The drain is sealing off! It's getting smaller.

The Water Lady's window was closing, and soon her world—and the access to Rebecca—would be slam shut with it.

He must hurry!

Harvey resurfaced and sat by the pool again, mulling the situation over. He grabbed the pool manual off the table and opened to the dog-eared page, confirming that the drain diameter was fourteen inches.

He ran into the garage and fetched a ruler from his toolbox, then dove back down to the drain. He wasn't sure, but it looked like it had shrunk even more since he had just been there!

He measured its diameter.

It was now just six inches!

He resurfaced, dried himself off, and put on his windbreaker.

He sat at the table and worried about how he was going to squeeze though the small drain to reunite with his beloved little daughter?

He then fell into a deep sleep, exhaustion having overcome him.

Harvey awoke, upset with himself that he had dozed off during his vigil. He glanced down at the drain.

The blue color under the grid was gone! Furthermore, the bubbles coming from the drain were larger!

Grabbing his mask and iron, Harvey dove to the drain and again pried off the grid.

At last, there she was! Rebecca's face appeared in the small hole!

Her sweet lips were visible just beyond the opening. He squeezed his face as far as he could into the hole, his lips just touching hers. He frantically tore his face away, seeing strands of her golden hair floating up to caress his nose.

He crammed his hand into the drain, but only part of it and a few fingers could fit. He felt her nose! He yanked his hand away as he realized that he was running out of air.

Rebecca's little hand then reached up to him, jutting out of the dark hole, just like in her painting— only his wife's hand was absent.

He grasped Rebecca's hand as she pulled him into the drain. Harvey, thrashing and kicking and short of oxygen, crammed his hand into the hole with all his might, following hers back down into the drain.

He could feel her sweet touch as he fought and fought to get inside.

He thrashed and kicked for what seemed like an eternity, and then . . . he ran out of oxygen.

In a matter of seconds, Harvey was completely still in the cold water.

Finally, he was at peace.

Rachael lay on her bed, sobbing. She had decided on a divorce, but still had her doubts. She wished that Harvey would come to bed.

It was almost morning, and the full moon had given way to the sun's insipient rays, filtering through the dew-drenched window with golden strands. At first, she thought it was a dream, and then she was sure that is was morning.

Or, was it?

She heard Rebecca's sweet giggles, mixed with Harvey's infectious laughter as she lay there in a murky twilight. Of course, it was a dream.

She slowly rose from her bed, throwing on her silk robe. Rachael looked out the window to the pool, its light still on.

She screamed. She screamed again.

Harvey's body floated face down in the pool, motionless.

She dashed out to the pool, diving into the water, pulling him to the side and then onto the shallow steps. He didn't budge.

He was stiff, and rigor mortis had set in. He was too heavy to get out of the pool, so she turned him over with a great effort, trying mouth-to-mouth resuscitation.

Oddly, his mouth had frozen into a smile.

It was useless. She knew he was dead.

She dragged herself out of the pool and ambled back toward the house, weeping. On the way, she glanced down at the hateful drain . . .

She noticed that it wasn't a drain anymore at all, but a small crack! That's impossible, she thought.

Now, how could that have happened?

In the kitchen, she grabbed her phone to call 911. Then, she mulled things over.

Harvey had told her that Rebecca would be gone soon, and her world was closing off.

Then, the three paintings on the wall occupied her mind.

What about the earth stones, and the laughter she had heard, and now the smile on her dead husband's face? Finally, there was the disappearing pool drain!

No, it couldn't be, thought Rachael.

But, she *did* hear them laughing, she thought, as if they had been frolicking in the pool . . .

Rachael dashed to her master bedroom closet, throwing open the door. She lurched to the shelf, bending over to inspect it.

She cupped her face with hands, the urge to vomit and scream having seized her simultaneously.

There they were, lying on the middle shelf.

Rumpled, used, not as she had left them, and one article definitely not even having been there before, there they rested, as she stood petrified, gasping for breath. Her mind raced.

They are soaking wet, too, as if they had just been in the pool!

She took them in her shaking hands.

Rebecca's red bathing suit, her glitter-lined goggles, and Harvey's oval, brown-framed watch—the one that his father had left him—all rested in her trembling hands—wet!

She shot out of the closet like a cannon—racing to the pool.

"Wait—take me with you!"

Rachael reached the pool and saw that the drain had disappeared almost entirely.

"I'm sorry! Don't leave me here! Don't leave me behind!"

She dove in the pool and down to the tiny crevice that was once the pool drain.

She thrashed and fought, jamming her hand into the small crack with all her might to force entry into the world of the Water Lady and her beloved daughter and husband.

Her fingers then got caught . . .

The tall, black policeman—Jim Wilson—pushed back his officer's cap over his grey hair and frowned, looking up at the huge maple tree, the warm afternoon soon shining through its bare branches.

"The second floor at City Hall wants us to investigate." He pointed to the bottom of the empty pool, and then to the two covered bodies lying on the deck.

The young, blond officer next to Jim scribbled case notes on a small pad. "Three deaths in as many months. All in this damn pool. It's hard to believe these were all accidents—even harder to believe suicide—although those two had grieved the loss of the first victim—their little girl."

"How could they all be homicide?" added the black sergeant.

"What do we know about the neighbors?"

"Not much," answered Wilson. "What did the detective on the case say?"

"They want the Medical Examiner involved, that's all I know."

Wilson slapped the pool manual against his thigh, "Odd thing is though, the wife was found dead at the bottom of the deep end, with those welts around her fingers—as if they were caught in something down there. It looks to me like she drowned—she died in the pool—but we'll see what the M.E. finds."

"What's so odd about that—the welts I mean?"

"What the hell did she get her fingers caught *in*?" He looked down at the manual. "This thing says there's a drain—fourteen inches in diameter." Wilson pointed to the bottom of the pool. "Where is it? Not all pools have them these days, you know."

"What are you trying to say?"

The black policeman pulled out a piece of paper from his uniform pocket. "This is a copy of the police report from the death of little Rebecca a few months ago. I'll read you something." He cleared his throat, and then continued. "'The deceased little girl's body was found expired over the pool *drain*.'" He put the book away. "They found her *at this address*, too."

"Easy, it's a mistake, that's all."

The inquisitive sergeant looked down wistfully at Harvey's body. "Mistake? Maybe. Nice folks. A nice guy—I met him recently."

"Too bad, a real sad case, Jim." The blond officer started to walk away, and then noticed something sitting on the deck table. "What the hell is that? Strange looking, isn't it?"

Jim Wilson took the beautiful, brown stone in his hands and rubbed it, as if it were an old friend.

"Yeah, I guess it is. It gives off heat. Here, feel."

"No thanks." The young officer put his hands up, as if it were radioactive.

"I saw one like this in Nam, back in the Army in seventy-two," said Wilson, "supposed to have special powers. One time in a battle—"

"—Yeah, sure," the younger cop laughed as he clapped his notebook shut, "a lot of hooey. I'm out of here for a late lunch." He walked off briskly.

Wilson watched the young officer leave, a hopeful young man in a hurry. He shook his head, feeling the warmth of the stone. "I'm not so sure it's hooey," he whispered. His thoughtful eyes glanced over at the bodies again, remembering the smile frozen on the male corpse, and the look of terror written on the expression of the wife.

Poor woman, he thought, she paid the price— for *not believing*.

He recalled that time long ago and far away. *I saw something strange back in those days. I took home a souvenir. It changed my life.*

Officer Wilson then pulled out his key chain, inspecting the bauble attached to the end of it. The round object at the end of the chain was also pretty.

It was black and grey with crosshatches and crooked stripes. "Yes sir, the *zebra onyx*," he mumbled as he looked over at the pool. "I hope at least two of them are together again, in a better place. They *believed*."

He heard a bird singing and the wind blowing through the old maple above him. Looking up, he smiled at the thick, sinewy branches, as if privy to its strange, whispery language warning him not to dwell too much upon his distant memory.

END.

Novelette Two: A Suitor
Part One:

A huge, red banner proclaimed: "May Day 1914—
Munich Laborers Unite Against Capitalists!"
Protesters, armed with clubs and chains, painted the
cobblestone streets of the Bavarian capitol red in their
own blood in Odeon's Square—in front of the
Feldherrnhalle—the Monument to the Field
Marshals.

One warring faction wore the dirty shirts and
soiled trousers of the trade unionists, and the other—
students from the sword-dueling fraternities—sported
the Prussian-blue tunics and scarred faces of the
monarchists. Bystanders, milling along the parade
route, stunned by the torn knuckles and smashed
noses of the combatants, hadn't noticed a fracas of a
different kind just beyond the crowd.

Two ruffians dragged a young girl wearing a
silk bonnet and a sashed, muslin dress into a nearby
alley, the feisty victim swinging her purse wildly in
self-defense.

She kicked and screamed as one mugger
grabbed her by her graceful neck and golden braids,
while the other—his meaty arms clamped around her
thin waist—helped to whisk her off into the dark
alley.

In a flash, they had carried her away, throwing
her to the ground behind a deserted news kiosk—her
purse opened and emptied—her dress hiked . . .

The quick eye of the gaunt and shabbily
dressed young man entering the alley from the other
direction spotted the crime in progress, as his husky,
bald friend stood at his side.

Kicking the one assailant in the groin, while his huge friend took the other man by the scruff of his neck, the two perpetrators were subdued, and then they broke and ran.

The lean youth with the shabby, dark overcoat and straight, unruly black hair helped the young lady off the dirty gravel. She straightened her torn dress and disheveled hair while the Good Samaritan picked up her purse and shagged its strewn contents, returning the articles to her with a chivalrous bow.

His bald sidekick—sporting greasy overalls and a red tattoo of an iron cross on his muscular forearm—smiled reassuringly at the distraught victim.

The man in the overcoat pushed back the tussle of hair, "There, there—" he gently patted her shoulder, "—I hope you are not hurt badly, Fraulein. It is fortunate that my friend Grab and I happened along." He looked into her tearstained eyes, "Are you all right?"

His large, radiant, light-blue eyes—eyes that looked *through* you, not *at* you—reassured her with sincerity and a hint of mirth.

"Yes, I'm all right. Thank you both—very much indeed, kind sirs."

She took a step, teetering a bit on her shiny, high-heeled shoes. Her smooth, finely manicured hands shook, "I must go home now. Papa shall be waiting for me."

"You're welcome, young Miss." The bald hulk blurted in deep tones, his toothless smile broadening.

With a dazed stare, she eyed the tall rows of dilapidated apartments lining the narrow alleyway. They blocked the sun, and tainted the air with their overflowing trashcans and sewers.

"What hour is it?" she asked.

"It's getting late, Fraulein," responded the hungry-looking man in the overcoat. "I shall escort you home. You look shaken."

The hollow-cheeked young fellow definitely had an air about him, she thought, as she stared at his filthy shoes with the big holes.

"I am of modest means, to be sure Fraulein, but no harm will come to you," he said. "You may trust me, be assured!"

She blushed.

He's so sensitive, as if he knows what I'm thinking. I do hope I didn't hurt his feelings. I didn't mean to stare at his shabby clothes.

She took an instant liking to this modest, scrawny young peasant with the surprising formality and grand manner—and the uncanny intuition.

"Yes, I *do* trust you," she declared with studied conviction. "I trust you *entirely*."

His face had a sensitive look to it, an artistic look, she thought.

"I am gratified, Fraulein."

Of medium height, he stood stiffly. He spoke in a pleasing, steady voice that had a scratchy but robust quality—a *reassuring* voice. A pert mouth, a short and fleshy nose, and a clean, smooth-shaven jawline suggested that he was of decent stock, if not from prosperous people.

"Escort me home, please sir, it's not far," requested the fair victim as she limped down the dark alley. "Do you think we should summon the police?"

"No, I think not. With the crowds out today, finding the scoundrels will be hard." He waved away his burly companion. "You may leave us now, Grab."

The bald hulk nodded in obedience to his friend—much as a butler would—as he took his leave.

The stranger with the greasy overcoat held out his arm to the lovely maiden, which she grasped, her gait assisted as they departed.

"Steady yourself, Fraulein, you had a terrible shock."

"My Christian name is Francesca." She felt a little pain in her knee where she had landed on the ground, "Francesca *Schmidt*. And *you*?"

The scruffy young man, walking with a proud carriage, didn't smile, but his pale-blue eyes shined like beacons. "You may call me *Audi*, Fraulein Schmidt. That is what my friends call me."

"Audi—is that all?"

"—Just, Audi."

"May I ask how old you are, Audi?"

She didn't know why she asked him that, except that he seemed so mature for his apparent years. She sensed in him a deep thinker who searched for a purpose in life.

"I am twenty-five years. And yourself?"

"I am twenty."

He seemed so gallant, yet sensitive, and *vulnerable,* completely unlike the typical young men of her class.

He had saved her from a fate worse than death at the hands of the scum who had accosted her. They ambled together, arm in arm, toward her papa's mansion—to a fashionable district of Munich.

"It is terrible, Audi. Last week I saw three bodies on the street after the anarchists battled the police."

Avoiding the large avenues with the big horse-drawn carriages, and, worse yet, the hordes of newfangled auto-cars that seemed to have taken over the public thoroughfares, they discussed many topics, almost as though they had known each other for years.

"What do you think of such things?" she asked. "Terrible fights are happening every day on the streets. There is always talk of war with France. If my sweet mother were still alive today, she'd be mortified—"

"—Well, Fraulein, I'm an artist, not a political man. I am not bothered by them much unless they bother me."

He dug into his pocket and pulled out a sketch of a building, handing it to her as they walked.

They had chatted nonstop for half an hour, not noticing the orange rays of the setting sun giving way to twilight.

"Ah, the Munich City Hall!" she exclaimed as she examined his sketch. "The likeness is true. Is the man standing in front of the edifice the Lord Mayor?"

"No, just a man—to give the building perspective."

"But Audi, the man's face is odd. He has no expression."

He eyed her with his distant stare.

"What use do I have for people?

He gesticulated with a wide sweep of his hand.

"Buildings are what count! I want to paint the great structures of the world. Someday my work shall adorn the finest museums, pictures of great works that will last for a thousand years. I may even design them myself! I promise, Fraulein Schmidt."

"My goodness."

A bit lost for words, she handed him his picture back, whereupon he placed it in the pocket of the baggy trousers that crept through the crack of his filthy coat.

"I'm sure some day you'll be famous, Audi."

"Oh Fraulein Schmidt, forgive me for my outburst, but my heart is full of passion for my craft! I hope I do not sound rough."

"Not at all, Audi, I admire your dedication."

Francesca pointed to a huge, neoclassical, white-columned home with three, cream-colored stories—ornately trimmed in yellow—sitting rather like a giant cake along the street.

"Here we are. My house. Papa will be waiting."

Tugging him along, she led him to the tall, maple door with ornate lions etched in the wood, "I insist that you meet him . . ."

"What work do you have?" grumped Herr Schmidt, his suspicious eyes frisking every detail of Audi's shabby appearance as he sat behind his huge oak desk. "I can tell from your accent that you're not from these parts."

Francesca's father glared at the modest youth across his lavish study, which was adorned with heavy, cherry wood furniture and the newest electric lamps. Expensive Cranach paintings hung on the knotty pine, paneled walls.

Francesca and her young man sat in antique, Queen Anne style chairs, facing the desk behind which Francesca's inquisitive father sat.

"As I told you, Herr Schmidt, I'm a painter."

Francesca leaned forward in her chair, her voice strong with indignation. "Papa, this isn't an interrogation. Audi saved me—"

Herr Schmidt put his hand up so that he would not be interrupted, his eyes still fixed on the stranger.

"Who are your people, young man?"

Audi, who sat on the edge of his chair, looked at Francesca, who had washed and changed into a rustic, Bavarian style dress with shoulder straps, and an alpine-trimmed blouse with balloon-sleeves. "Go ahead Audi, my papa wants to get to know you."

The visitor cleared his throat. "I am from Vienna. My folks are deceased."

Francesca's kind eyes encouraged Audi. She nodded her head as he talked. "My father left me a small legacy to live on, sir. He was a lowly civil servant."

Herr Schmidt stood up from his desk—a tall, greying man—meticulously attired in a dark suit with a waist-chain and pocket watch.

"I see," he said in a softer voice. He took money out of the drawer of his desk. His penetrating, brown eyes nervously darted between his humble guest and his beautiful, gold-braided daughter.

"I thank you sir for coming to the aid of my sweet Francesca," he said as he walked around the desk, approaching Audi with a wad of bills in his outstretched hand.

"This is for your trouble—"

"—Papa!"

Francesca jumped out of her chair. "How dare you treat Audi like that? How rude! He's not your doorman!"

The visitor slowly rose from his chair, his red face complementing his smoldering blue eyes. "I assure you sir that I did not come here for remuneration!"

The young man took the bills and threw them on the floor. "I am a *German*, just as you are. Furthermore, I am a rising young man in my trade!"

Herr Schmidt's jaw dropped a bit as he shook his head, looking at Francesca sheepishly for forgiveness. "I meant no offense, dear fellow."

Francesca rushed to her father, taking his hand in hers as Audi stood his ground, erect and proud—definitely a youth with presence.

Herr Schmidt glanced at his guest, forcing himself to smile. "Please, Audi, I beg your pardon. My daughter, although headstrong, is a good judge of character. She prizes your friendship. I only wanted to—"

"—That is quite all right, I assure you."

Audi looked around the richly appointed room, his eyes shining. His manner grew more confident, even superior, as if he took for granted the trappings of polite society.

"I admire your paintings, Herr Schmidt, and your house is a fine example of neoclassical design."

"Thank you."

"I see you have a Cranach hanging," said Audi.

"Yes."

"The son or the father?"

Herr Schmidt cast him a look of regard.

"The son."

Audi picked up the bills and handed them to Francesca's father.

"So, you know architecture and art, young man?"

"A little."

Where did you learn this, if I may ask?"

Audi hesitated, and then said with conviction. "I had connections with the School of Architecture in Vienna. I don't think they fully appreciated my talent."

Herr Schmidt, his smile a bit more relaxed, walked up to Audi and put his arm around him, "That's not unusual, my boy. I'm an architect, and I know the feeling. Seriously, is there nothing I can do for you for saving my daughter's honor?"

Francesca walked over to Audi and gave him a reassuring smile. "Papa, I've seen Audi's art." She winked at her young friend. "It's really quite powerful. Can you commission him to paint a likeness of our home in watercolor?"

"Excellent idea," chimed Herr Schmidt. He smiled at the young man. "Well, Audi, what do you think of that? My daughter has a great idea."

Audi's eyes roamed the room, moving from the autographed photo of the Kaiser hanging on the wall back to the grateful father.

"I shall accept, Herr Schmidt."

They shook hands.

Francesca beamed with delight.

Herr Schmidt then frowned, his balding head nodding as if agreeing with himself.

"Now that I see you are all right, my dear, bid the maid to fetch Captain Von Braun of the Munich police—an old friend."

Audi's face tightened at the name of the policeman.

"He must come straight away," continued Francesca's father. "We must file a formal report so that the culprits who assailed you shall be caught."

"I must take my leave now, Herr Schmidt," interjected Audi, "farewell." He took Francesca's hand and kissed it, "Dearest Miss, I bid you goodbye as well." He headed for the door.

She escorted him out. Herr Schmidt watched the nervous young man closely as Audi disappeared with his daughter from his study. He put his hand to his chin as his eyes narrowed.

"I can sell three of your sketches for every landscape watercolor you make, Audi, for three marks a piece. You do the math. At five marks per watercolor—that take much longer to produce— you'll starve if you stick to paintings."

Goldfarb took a drag on one of his stem-handled cigarettes, brushing the ash from his crumpled, stained shirtsleeve. "Now do you want to make business, or don't you?"

"I must consider the possibilities, my friend," answered Audi.

Goldfarb raised his nasal voice above the din of the clanging pots and clashing dishes. "I thought I just did that." His quick, black eyes glanced around the sea of crowded tables in the soup-kitchen courtyard—the communal slopping hole for the flophouse tenants. "Is this a deal or what?"

"You want me to sketch tourist traps from postcards, and then peddle them at the Main Train Station. That is beneath me, Herr Goldfarb!"

Audi sat across the dirty table from his peddler friend, slurping his soup between sentences, hungrily eyeing the stale bun sitting by his bowl. "You are good at business, Goldfarb. I am good at art."

The salesman took another drag from his cigarette, pushing away his plate of red cabbage. "You give me twenty sketches a week and I'll sell them all, and keep only one-fourth the take."

"That's a lot of work." Audi scraped his bowl with his spoon. "I'm a busy man. Besides, I haven't the pencils."

"You sit around and read old newspapers and library books all day, then go to the opera and blow all your money on third class seats. You and your Wagner! Sketch Audi, sketch I say!"

Goldfarb twirled his mustache with one hand and pulled on his blue suspender with the other, considering his next move. "Here are a few marks for pencils," he said as he dug into his pocket and placed a few coins next to Audi's soup bowl. "Now, is it a deal?"

Grab strode up to the table, which had plenty of room for another person. He glared down at Goldfarb, and then made a show of plopping his bowl of soup down upon the empty table next to theirs.

Audi smiled. "Grab over there doesn't like you, Goldfarb. I don't know why. He chooses another table."

The bald giant bent his massive head over his soup after he sat down, his bull neck straining the button on his collar. He picked up the steaming bowl and sucked down its contents with ample sound effects.

Audi stood up and straightened his ever-present, black overcoat—the only coat that he owned. "You people are good at the selling, Goldfarb. There is no question of that."

"*You* people?" Goldfarb shook his head. "What do you mean, Audi, *you people*?"

"Salesmen! That's what I mean. Tell you what, I'll give you two sketches, Herr Goldfarb, and we'll see what happens."

Audi looked over at Grab, who wiped the spilled soup from his neck with his sleeve. The huge wrestler burped and then scowled—the look in his eye forbidding.

"I bid you goodbye, gentleman," said Audi as he left with a spring in his step, as if amused by the tension between his two fellow lodgers.

The forceful blow of steam from the huge train hit Audi's little table of displayed wares as the shining locomotive screeched to a halt, its powerful engines roaring. Audi dashed to pick up one of his prized watercolors—an emotionless study of the Munich Grand Opera House—that had blown onto the sooty floor of the Main Train Station gangplank.

He winced at the acrid scent of the coal dust as he navigated the stampede of exiting passengers streaming out the train's door. The roar of the train's engine deafened him. Holding up his watercolor to the arriving travelers, his art didn't receive so much as a curious glance.

Who *had* given his artwork some attention was the pesky cop who had made his rounds of the station not ten minutes before, eyeing Audi's setup with open distain.

It was only a matter of time before he would rap his baton on the fragile little card table. Then, he would order Audi to find another venue for his merchandizing, as he had done countless times before.

Audi spotted a potential customer, one of the last commuters exiting the train. He held the watercolor up to a tall man with a loud tie—a tourist wearing one of the new American-style hats that he had seen in a magazine—as the visitor rushed past him with a suitcase. One of those new, portable cameras hung around his neck.

"Please, would you like to see my art?" asked Audi with a grim expression.

The man scowled, flicking his cigar ash on Audi's foot as he sped past. "No, I would not!" he blasted in a thick accent.

Audi, discouraged and confused, hadn't in fact sold anything for days. He couldn't understand why people didn't see how *special* his work was—how *pure* it was.

Unlike the newfangled cubist, impressionist, Dadaist, and other modern crap that artists hawked all day and night around the Munich tourist spots, his style had character and *nobility*—and it actually *looked like* what it represented. Ever since his grade school days, he had been unappreciated, considering his teachers at best lunatics.

The discouraged young man glanced back at his shabby table of watercolors. A chill of apprehension shot down his spine. There was one consolation. He had sold a small sketch of the old *Frauenkirche* yesterday—for two marks.

A short man, wearing a white fedora hat with a dark band, and a long, white overcoat, stood next to his table, furtively glancing at Audi, and then back down at his paintings. To Audi, he seemed to only *pretend* that he was interested in his work.

The shifty, black eyes of the stranger darted behind the light-reflecting facade of his thick, slightly beveled eyeglasses, which—at that angle and lighting—gave the stranger the unsettling appearance of having more than two eyes.

The man really didn't look like he was interested in his paintings at all, thought Audi darkly, but *something else. Who is this strange fellow? Could he be following me?* As soon as the man in the white hat left, Audi quickly packed up and left to move his inventory to another spot.

"I would like to have a word with Audi, if you don't mind," said Francesca in a determined voice.

"Oh, yes" said the elderly, pleasantly trim woman, brushing off the crumbs from her apron and opening the door wide for the fine lady to enter. "The skinny young man living on the top floor—the one with the books and paintings. He's in."

The pink-cheeked young lady wearing the festive, yellow-silk dress and golden braids surveyed the flophouse with a grimace of slight distaste, noting the broken window of the tailor shop next door.

"Thank you, Matron."

"You're welcome young Miss. I'll show you to the waiting room, and he'll be down directly to meet you."

These furnished little studios on the *Schleissheimstrasse* housed disreputable elements, Francesca recalled. Her papa would be furious had he known that she was there. The matron carefully studied the young lady as Francesca walked past her.

Observing the refinery of her hoity-toity guest, she smiled with crooked teeth and a knowing wink, nodding as if they shared a dirty secret.

"Who should I say is calling, Fraulein?"

"Francesca . . ."

Francesca didn't care to sit on the dirty chair in the dreadful waiting room. The base smell of the musty carpet revolted her. She then noticed something that lifted her spirits.

A sketch of the Main Train Station hung on the dirty wall.

"You like it Fraulein Francesca?"

She twirled around.

"Very much." She smiled at the young man who had drawn the sketch. Audi stood at the foot of the stairs, dressed in his same old, black overcoat, with the familiar tassel of dark hair falling over his forehead.

"I like it even more than your City Hall piece."

He walked over to her and kissed her hand. "The matron gives me a reduced rent . . ." Then, he bit his tongue, as if realizing that he was divulging too much about his poverty. "It's nice to see you again. How did you find me?"

"It wasn't hard," she replied.

Francesca admired his confidence, and yet he seemed vulnerable—to her, an immensely attractive mix. She shook her finger at him in mock reproach, "You haven't honored our home with your commission as you promised. It's been weeks now. Papa still wants you to paint our house. He'll pay you fifty marks."

Audi shoved his hands in his pockets. He pulled them inside out, demonstrating to the young, beautiful girl that they were empty.

He smiled. "When do I start, dearest Miss?"

"Next week. And *please* call me Francesca!"

Audi looked at her, and then looked around at the shabby surroundings, then down at the floor with his head hanging low. "Are you sure you want me to do the commission, dearest Francesca?"

She wedged her hands on her narrow hips. "Look Audi, I want to tell you something right now. Don't feel bad that you live in this awful place."

She wagged her long, smooth finger at him. "That will pass! One day you'll live in a finer house than mine. You can rely on it. You have a certain quality that I cannot describe, but it *isn't* common. All right?"

Audi stood up straight again, his head high.

She took his arm and led him to the door. "And now, we have lunch at the Cafe Heck—my treat! That is, unless you already have plans."

Francesca smiled broadly at him.

Audi seemed lost for words.

"Yes," she insisted, "then it's on to the matinee at the Grand Opera House, my treat *also*. Wagner's *Siegfried* is playing!"

Audi, his eyes on fire with excitement, grabbed a pillow off the divan and twirled around the room. Clutching it to his chest, as if he were dancing a waltz in a grand ballroom, he hummed the music as his feet moved lightly over the dirty carpet.

Francesca clapped to the makeshift tune. She started twirling too, her yellow dress rising a bit to show her shapely, legs dressed in white stockings. She laughed so hard that a tear ran down her cheek.

Just then, the old Frau Matron entered the room, looking on the gay scene with a smile, clapping her hands. Audi stopped and looked at the elderly woman, blushing. Francesca stopped too. She cupped her mouth with her hands to muffle her giggles.

"Ah, to be young again!" The old Frau's eyes twinkled, no doubt with fond remembrance of her younger days.

Then, it was off to the Cafe Heck, and the famous Grand Opera House.

"You blushed, Audi. Back at the apartment, you turned red when the matron caught us dancing. *I've never seen a man blush before.*"

"I certainly did *not*. Women blush."

Francesca smiled at him. "Yes, it *is* so. You did."

The gentle, warm, late-morning breeze caught Francesca's silk dress just enough to make her sheer blouse levitate in the sun's gentle rays. They sipped their tea in the blue-and-white, English china cups, enjoying the spectacle of other guests in the tree-lined *biergarten* at the elegant Cafe Heck.

The scent of the cakes baking in the kitchen permeated the air. The green fluff of the chestnut trees swayed with the balmy gusts of wind.

Francesca dug into her deep, strawberry tart. Audi stuffed a Bavarian cream cake into his mouth with less than impeccable manners, as his vigilant eyes shifted to the middle aged, heavy-set man in the tailored suit seated at the table next to them. He wore a derby hat and a fine golden watch—on his wrist—in the new style. He reached into his coat pocket and then put his hand to his nose, snuffing his tobacco.

He's probably a banker, surmised Audi.

Then, Audi caught the headline of the newspaper that this prosperous-looking moneylender was reading over his morning coffee: "Serbian Nationalism On The Rise—Threat of War Looms."

Audi shook his head violently, his thoughts racing. *Mein Gott*! *Those Serbs are at it again!*

Francesca, her smile fading, noticed his grimacing. "Audi, what is wrong? That man over there next to us—do you know him?"

"No Fraulein Francesca. It's nothing."

Audi's gaze shifted to the fine ladies in their flowery, colorful dresses and round-brimmed, wide hats, who were busily conversing with their smug, bourgeois men. Many of the men sported the copycat, walrus mustaches of the German Emperor, Kaiser Wilhelm.

Audi winced at the monotony of it all.

"Did you know your parents well, Audi?"

He took a sip of his tea and paused to answer her question, his countenance guarded as his eyes glazed over in thought. "I loved my mother very much. She was ill—with cancer. I took care of her."

He wiped his mouth with the linen napkin.

"My father bullied me. He wanted me to work in his field." Audi's hand started to shake. His voice took on more gravel. "He never recognized my great gifts. My saintly mother did."

Francesca reached over the table and gently patted his hand. "Don't fret, my dear. It's a lovely day, isn't it?"

Audi stared at her distantly, his eyes the blue searchlights near the seas of his mind. "You remind me of my sacred mother—Madame."

Francesca smiled, and then it faded quickly. She looked into his eyes, and then removed her hand.

All of a sudden, there was the blaring sound of a marching band. Hundreds of grey-uniformed infantrymen—with rifles slung over their backs—had paraded from the *Odeonsplatz* down past the cafe.

Their shiny black boots pounded the cobblestone street as they goose-stepped to the martial beat of *Deutschland Uber Alles*. Francesca frowned when she saw the marching, but Audi's face lit up.

"Look at them, Fraulein Schmidt. Look at them!" He noticed Francesca's frown.

"Yes, Fraulein, I think I know what you mean. I agree. They think they are so *superior*."

Audi then jumped up from his chair and grabbed the mop standing against the wall next to their table. He ran to the end of the passing parade and got in line behind the last recruit.

Slinging the mop over his back, he goose-stepped with the rest of them, mocking their pomposity. Audi glanced over at Francesca, who gasped with delight.

She jumped up from the table too, and ran to Audi in the lineup, pulling him out.

"Audi! Stop it. They'll arrest you!" She convulsed with laughter.

They went back to the table.

The other patrons scowled at them.

"We'd better leave now. Besides, the matinee starts soon," she said. She couldn't stop giggling. Audi grinned mischievously.

She quickly paid the bill. They hurried out of the cafe to catch the show.

Gasping for breath, Francesca, with Audi at her side, pushed a ten-mark bill at the young lady in the box office and took the tickets. She handed one to Audi.

His eyes widened to large circles. "*Mein Gott*—dear Francesca—*first class* tickets to the opera *Siegfried*!"

"That's—that's . . . right," she responded with labored breathing.

"Are you all right, Fraulein?" He noted with alarm her physical distress.

"Yes—just tired, that's all—from our rush from the Cafe Heck."

Audi looked at her doubtfully. "I shall watch over you, dearest Miss."

He held out his arm to steady her. "Take my arm, please. We shall sit now."

He glanced up at the ornate spectacle of the Munich Grand Opera House as they entered its huge, gilded doors. They took their seats on the richly padded seats, glancing up at the elaborately detailed walls and ceiling artistry, and the hand-painted drop curtain in the front of the giant structure.

The huge, curved, ceiling beams, combined with the columns rising up on either side of the proscenium, suggested to Audi the opulence of the gilded age. The orchestra warmed up their instruments. Audi marveled at the rich acoustics as the multiple tiers of seats wrapped around them in cozy intimacy.

He had not been able to afford as many of the operas as he had in Vienna, even third class ones. This was only the second performance he had attended in Munich.

The room darkened. Francesca grabbed Audi's hand, which he reflexively moved to his lap.

He didn't like being touched.

As the opera played, Audi sank into a trance-like state, his eyes widening at the sight of the mighty swords, the winged helmets, and the beautiful, full-figured, blond amazons with the long, radiant golden braids.

To him, their allure was their virtue.

The music brought up something within him that he could only recall as resembling the feeling he had when he was twelve years old. At that time, a distant Aunt—visiting the family from Linz—had given him a bath, and cleaned him in areas that had been, until then, reserved only for him to clean.

The zenith of his rapture came in the third act, with the sensuous, overwhelming, crescendo decrescendo music attending the riveting climax of the opera. Siegfried entered the "Ring of Fire," emerging upon Brunnhilde's rock. When he removed her armor, he discovered that she was a *woman*—a creature that he had never seen before.

Audi's breathing became heavier as he witnessed Siegfried—on the glorious stage—kissing his love, and awakening her from a deep slumber. Falling in love with Siegfried—Brunnhilde renounced the gods so that she could be with her mortal lover.

The tall, blond soprano who played Brunnhilde then sang the golden aria, "*Ewig War Ich*!" Audi grabbed the arms of his chair as he listened to the celestial woman sing. He closed his eyes.

He slowly stood up from his chair.

Carried away, he started singing in sync with the young lady on the stage—knowing the libretto by heart. Francesca nudged his shoulder, suppressing a laugh with her hand to her mouth.

He kept on singing.

She tried to pull him back down in his seat with no result. The other patrons grumbled at this shabbily dressed upstart. They screamed at him to shut up and sit down.

The enraptured young man then opened his eyes when the aria had finished. Audi then looked around him with a surprised look on his face—obviously recalling where he was.

Out of the corner of his eye, he could see an usher approaching. He quickly plopped back down in his chair, silent once more. The opera over, Francesca stood up and tugged Audi out of his chair.

As they quickly left the theater, Audi's translucent eyes locked upon Francesca's. "Tell me, Fraulein Schmidt, is there any more proof that you need of the superiority of the German soul?"

"I don't have the money for sketchpads, Herr Goldfarb."

"Here Audi, you need your tools." He handed the ascetic Austrian a fiver.

"I cannot accept, sir, but I thank you just the same."

His friend left it on the table.

"You can pay me from your profits from the sketches if you like. I sold the two you gave me. Have you thought any more about our deal?"

"I don't know. I like my paintings. However, as you say, they're not selling."

Audi reached down, picking up a large painting leaning against the leg of the thick, oak table at which they sat. He placed it gently in front of them after wiping its surface with a rag.

"See here, Goldfarb. Are you telling me you cannot sell this beautiful watercolor? Everyone loves architecture, do you not agree?" Audi held his painting up from the table for his associate to see.

The young salesman twirled his thin mustache as he studied the architecturally sound picture with the bluish tones and geometrically monotonous straight edges.

"No, not really Audi."

He lit one of his stem-handled cigarettes.

"Maybe *famous* buildings, but this is just a plain *residence*."

His quick black eyes studied the label on the piece. "It's even named 'The *Courtyard* of the Old Residency in Munich'. I don't see much of a courtyard."

Audi put down his painting.

He scowled at the patron eating at the table next to them in the giant, flag-draped *Festhaal*, located on the upper floor of the famous Hofbrau House.

The grotesquely fat man smacked his lips while devouring his sausages and kraut. Audi sickened from the smell of seared animal flesh. "I beg your pardon, Herr Goldberg—"

"—Audi—the name's Gold*farb*—"

"Excuse me, Goldfarb—but I think you don't know what you are talking about."

Audi studied his companion's new suit and gold watch. There were no stained sleeves this time. He then looked down at the holes in his old shoes sticking out from under the table.

He felt a pang of envy.

Besides, he was loosing too much weight from not enough to eat. "Tell me again, Goldfarb, what can do for me?"

Goldfarb turned his head and blew out his smoke, then put the cigarette down in the tray and snuffed it. "Sorry Audi, I forgot you don't like to smoke."

"That is quite all right, Herr Goldberg."

"Well Audi, it's like this . . ."

Just then, a soldier sitting two tables away started yelling at a young man with a long mustache, who sat over his open book at the table next to the man in uniform. Audi overheard a bit of the argument, in which the student had called the soldier a "dirty warmonger," claiming that he, the student, was a devout Marxist.

The soldier stood up from his chair, his hands clenched in tight fists—his face red with rage. The man with the mustache jumped up too, knocking over his table, a dozen empty beer steins falling to the ground and smashing.

The burly man in the uniform took his empty beer stein—by its long handle—and hit it against the edge of his table, making it into a sharp blade. He lunged at the student, grabbing him by the hair, running the blade down the young man's face. Blood gushed as the victim fell to the floor.

The bouncer rushed over to the table and threw them both out the door. Audi and Goldfarb, not in the least disturbed by the violence, resumed their conversation as if nothing had happened.

Goldfarb took out a pad and pencil from his coat pocket. "You sketch twenty per week. You charge a certain amount. I cover all expenses, and we sell at the Opera House and the Main Train Station."

The pool of blood on the ground formed a tiny river, slowly snaking its way over to their table. "I take twenty percent—less than I said before," continued Goldfarb. "You sketch only famous tourist sights. What we don't sell, I buy from you for half price. What you say?"

"Well . . ." The fact was, the business-minded Goldfarb impressed Audi, and the deal sounded fair. "I'll think about it."

"In the mean time, Audi, please take the fiver to cover your materials." The agent nodded toward the note he left lying on the table.

"All right. The fiver is mine." Audi scooped up the note and put it in his overcoat pocket. He needed his dinner, and for the cost of materials for the commission on Francesca's house.

"And buy yourself a new overcoat!" blurted Goldfarb.

"I think you are seeing too much of this young vagabond from Vienna, my dear."

Herr Schmidt pounded his fist on his desk as Francesca sat on the sofa in his study, tears streaming down her face. "Let's face facts. He's as common as dirt. I appreciate what he did for us, but let us not go overboard here. His commission started last week, so he'll be handsomely paid soon—and he is gone."

Noticing her response, he rose from his desk and strode over to his daughter, patting her shoulder gently. "My dear . . ."

"Papa, he's not a vagabond. He's a great artist. He does have some rough edges, I agree. But, so does an uncut diamond."

"Well, he's no diamond." Francesca's father wrung his hands and shook his head, then sat down beside her.

"Oh papa . . ."

He kissed her gently upon her forehead.

"Look," he urged in hushed tones, "we barely know Audi. We've only known him two months. Let's exercise discretion, that's all."

He handed her his handkerchief. "Now, wipe your pretty eyes, my dear, all will be well."

Francesca patted her eyes dry and then handed his hankie back to him.

"Yes, Papa."

A light rap on the closed study door broke the momentary silence. Herr Schmidt looked at the door with irritation.

"Yes, Greta, come in!"

Francesca rose from the sofa and walked to the desk to straighten her father's mess of ashes that he had left from his pipe.

A heavy, elderly woman with a black-and-white maid's uniform entered the room with her hands folded apologetically.

"It's Professor Zimmerman, Your Honor. He's come to see young Francesca."

Francesca rolled her eyes.

He nodded to the maid. "Yes, Greta, I forgot. Show him in please."

Herr Schmidt looked at his daughter as Francesca frowned at him.

"Bring him here Greta," he ordered.

The maid left, leaving the door open a crack.

"'*You forgot*'. Sure Papa!"

Francesca glared at the door, as if a leopard would sneak through any moment. "I told you not to invite him here! You invited that old fuddy-duddy over here many times before, and I told you that I didn't want to see him."

Herr Schmidt put his finger to his mouth, "Not so loud, he'll hear you." Then, he wagged it at her. "Now Francesca, he's a distinguished Professor of Architecture at the University of Munich. I like him. He's determined. And you'll be twenty-one soon. Besides, he's not so old."

Herr Schmidt moved towards the door, ready to welcome the gentleman caller.

"He's forty-three! His breath smells like onions! And he's already asked for my hand twice."

"He's a good catch by anybody's book. He's also a friend of our exalted Monarch. Let's hope he tries a *third* time."

Just then, the door opened wider, and there stood Professor Johannes Fredrick Zimmerman, his countenance weighty.

"Good day, Herr Schmidt," he uttered stiffly.

Zimmerman, tall and lean with broad shoulders, wasn't built like a frump.

However, a double chin, his grey, pork chop whiskers, coupled with his ridiculously enormous walrus mustache in emulation of the Kaiser, countered his fine physique. Bristles of grey hair pointed at right angles directly from the skin under his nostrils.

"Francesca, I hope you are well," his commanding, baritone voice boomed as he marched into the center of the study, pompously bowing.

"May I have a word with you alone, my dear, with your father's permission of course?"

Zimmerman's earnest, bovine, brown eyes, and his expensive, tan-leather riding clothes, suggested the country squire on a holiday. He stepped closer to Francesca as Herr Schmidt quickly exited the room, the scheming father giving his esteemed colleague a furtive wink as he passed.

"The room's all yours, Herr Professor."

"Francesca," he said in a brassy, somber tone. "I'll get right to the point. I feel I must save you— from yourself."

Francesca inched away from him, taking a seat behind her father's desk, leaning back in his chair. She folded her arms, as she had seen her father do during many heated conversations. She stuffed her father's old pipe in her mouth. "Explain that remark, sir."

Zimmerman's eyes widened with surprise at the foreign sight of a lady biting on a pipe. "That young man you're cavorting with is not for you." He put his hands on his hips. "An *artist*! My goodness, what are you thinking of? And he's a *foreigner* to boot—not to mention penniless."

"You sound like someone I know. But, I love *that* person—my father. I don't love you."

"You'll love me too, some day—"

"—When herrings waltz."

"What future can you have? He's an uneducated cad—and please take that ridiculous pipe out of your mouth!"

Francesca shot up from her chair.

She quickly lit the pipe, blowing blue smoke at her tormentor. "He's not a cad!" She coughed.

"I suspect his character."

She emptied the contents of the pipe into the ashtray. "Suspect all you want. Now leave this instant—"

"—When I'm ready!"

She threw the empty pipe at him. He ducked.

Zimmerman moved closer to Francesca, holding his hands up to her—pleading. "Forgive me if I offended you, my precious." His voice softened with his new tack. "I want you for my wife. Please say yes!"

"Your wife? What would she want with me?"

Zimmerman's eyes registered shock at the outrageous insolence of her base sense of humor. Francesca rushed to the door, throwing it open.

"Please leave!"

Zimmerman made his way slowly to the door. He stopped next to her as she looked away from him.

"I may *look* like an old fogey, but I assure you I'm the best shot in Germany."

Francesca turned her head back toward him, her startled eyes meeting his.

"Yes, that's right dear. It's been a while since I've used my dueling pistols, but that doesn't mean I forgot how. I'll defend your honor with my life!"

Francesca saw that his mouth was contorted as he spoke, "You can tell *him* that," continued the professor, "him, or any other scum that pretends your hand! From here on out, Fraulein, I request that you do exactly as I tell you!"

The big man stomped out of the house. She knew he meant business. Her Papa had been unaware of this insane man's vile temper. She was in fact deathly afraid of him.

What was she to do? She thought that she was doomed.

I loathe him!

Francesca's breathing suddenly quickened. She put her hands to her heart. Loud wheezes came from her chest.

Herr Schmidt rushed in. "You're upset, my dear. Forgive me! It's your asthma attack again."

He led Francesca to the sofa and helped her lie down. He unbuttoned her collar and fanned her with a piece of paper.

Herr Schmidt glanced back at the door. "Greta!"

The maid appeared.

"Fetch Doctor Pavlov, the Russian lung doctor! First, boil some foxglove tea!"

Herr Schmidt gently stroked his daughter's hair. "Courage, my dear, you'll be all right in no time."

Presently, the maid brought the tea, and then ran from the house to fetch the doctor, who happened to live nearby.

As Greta exited the front gait, she didn't see the short man behind the large birch tree—the one with the white fedora hat with the dark band, and the white overcoat.

As he spied on the house through his thick eyeglasses, he took meticulous notes.

Thousands of people milled about the streets. Anarchists and Marxists battled with Monarchists and Capitalists. Placards and signs spewed hatred and aggression. Violent prejudices that had been bubbling over in fits and starts gave rise to more convulsive bouts of violence in front of monuments and museums.

The newspaper headlines hit like a tornado:

"ARCHDUKE FRANZ FERDINAND OF AUSTRIA AND WIFE ASSASSINATED!"

"SERBIAN AND 'YOUNG BOSNIAN' ELEMENTS IMPLICATED IN MURDERS!"

"JUNE 28, 1914—A DAY OF TREACHERY"

"AUSTRIA AND GERMAN ALLY BRISTLE FOR WAR; RUSSIANS BACK SERBIA"

Part Two:

Audi lay in his crumpled, coffee-stained bed, rummaging through newspapers, as was his custom when he could afford to buy them. His face froze in indignation; his eyes shinned with excitement.

Maybe, here's my chance, he thought.

Serbians killed the Archduke!

I am an artist, but a German first.

My *real* country needs me—Germany!

He threw on his reeking, black overcoat and trotted down the rickety stairs to the soup kitchen in the courtyard, careful not to go by the matron's desk in case she nagged him for his rent.

In the courtyard, Grab and his cronies greeted him as they milled about the slop tables. They slurped their porridge and brandished their clubs and whips—some with pistols too.

Grab stood up from his table as Audi approached. At Grab's table sat Georg, an unemployed butcher with a missing finger, who loved the Kaiser; Karl, a poor grocer, who refused sell potatoes to Socialists; old Hans—a toothless veteran of the 1871 War with France—who kept his rifle loaded for any Slavs and Russians that he might meet; and Grab himself, who often carried a dog-whip with him in case he met foreigners who wore those funny hats.

All these men had attired themselves in comfortable Bavarian clothing that their anticipated belligerence would require; always with *lederhosen* and leather suspenders, knee socks, loose white shirts, and quaint alpine hats with little feathers stuck stylishly in them.

Audi took his seat with this rabble, brooding and watchful. His mesmerizing, blue eyes scanned the solemn faces of his entourage, many of whom he had become, if not friends, tacit comrades with.

Grab's massive, bald, head turned toward the corner of the room, his porcine eyes narrowing and his yellow teeth clenched—he had spotted something. An unemployed, young loan broker, who had always taken meals by himself, huddled over his coffee and rolls in the far corner table.

He was thought of by the rest of the men present as somewhat of a dandy, and hailed from Prussia, where the central government resided in Berlin. His worn but well tailored clothing and carefully tended, blond hair never failed to irritate the flophouse tenants. A poor man, like themselves, he nevertheless had youth and prospects.

Grab strode past the bubbling soup cauldrons spewing their bacon and beef-lard odors. He approached the young man who ate quietly.

The dandy looked up from his coffee, noticing Grab staring at him. He continued with his meal.

"Money handler!" snorted Grab.

The young man ignored him.

"Usurer!"

He ignored him again.

"Prussian scum!"

Audi slowly stood up, watching the spectacle closely.

"I'm a Bavarian—and I hate the stinking Prussians! Go home!" yelled Grab.

Nothing happened—

This time, Grab grabbed his prey under his armpits, picked the hapless lender up from his table—kicking and screaming—, and carried him over to the soup cauldron like he was throwing away a child's doll. He quickly got his victim in a headlock and submerged his head into the scalding soup.

Just before the loan broker's legs stopped thrashing, Audi rushed over to Grab and pushed him off the young Prussian. The man, pulling his head out of the soup, gasped for air, screaming with pain. His scalded face covered in soup—he staggered out of the courtyard.

"We are all brothers here. We are all Germans," said Audi in a forceful, scratchy voice as his mesmerizing eyes scanned the men sitting at the tables. At first a bit unsure of himself, the young artist continued his oration with his hands moving in rhythm with his commanding voice.

"The foreign elements want us to devour each other! The enemy is clever. Do you not understand: 'Divide and conquer'? Have you not heard that saying, gentlemen?"

Grab hung his head low.

The rest of the men, awestruck, slowly rose to their feet. Some clapped.

"Recruits and volunteers form a line—remove your shirts and strip to the waist!"

Audi stood next to the sign, in front of a uniformed man, who wore a grey tunic with red trim and shoulder bars. His mustache and short-cropped, red hair—with his compact, trim physique that was accented by his thick, brass-buckled belt—lent a crisp look to this corporal in the Kaiser's service.

He ruffled his papers as he sat at the messy recruiting table, under huge photos of Kaiser Wilhelm and the Crown Prince of Bavaria, which hung on the beige wall behind him.

"We received your request for an intake appointment. I am Corporal Stein. You are applying to join the List Regiment then, is that correct?"

Audi stood in his filthy overcoat, his hair cascading over his forehead, his look hungry as ever as he answered.

"Yes."

"Yes *sir*," Stein corrected him.

He stood to attention. "Yes sir!"

"Your papers are not in order. You are a foreigner, is that not correct?"

"I am from Austria, across the river from Germany, if that is what you mean, *Herr Hauptman*."

"Nevertheless, there are some irregularities. Austria has its own draft requirements."

"I am a *German*, sir!"

"Don't take that tone with me, young man."

"Yes sir." Audi's face turned red as his jaw tightened—his phosphorescent, blue eyes glowing.

"I have your immigration papers here—those ones we were able to obtain, anyway. There are some questions to resolve. Is that not correct?"

"Yes sir."

"You have thirty days to resolve those questions, or you *will* be deported. You have until the third day of August. It that understood?"

"Yes Corporal Stein!"

"You are dismissed!"

Audi saluted jauntily, then hung his head low and started to turn away. The corporal scratched his head. He took the measure of the earnest young applicant.

"Wait!"

The recruiter's hard, green eyes softened.

He stood up from the table and closely examined a few forms that he had picked out of his basket. He picked up a pen and signed one of them.

"Young man, you have *two* options. You can petition the Crown Prince for a special dispensation— that expires in a maximum of thirty days from today also, or you can . . . find yourself a nice German girl and get married! Here are the necessary papers for both."

The recruiter shoved the papers in Audi's outstretched hand. "Of course, maybe they'll be an outright war declared by then. That may help you. The news is bad—you never know."

As Audi left, the short man in the white fedora hat with the dark band crept out of the back room, and walked up to Corporal Stein.

"That's the one—lean and hungry. He goes by the name '*Audi*' so-and-so, but our department in the police force thinks he's using an alias—a name resembling his real name in Austria. We believe he escaped the draft there, and is therefore here in Germany illegally."

"I see. You are with the Department of Uninvited Aliens, is that right?"

"That is correct, sir. I report to Captain von Braun."

At the mention of that name, the corporal pursed his lips and nodded. "Von Braun is well respected."

"Very much so, Corporal."

Corporal Stein shrugged. "This young man seems a decent sort. We always need brave men who want to fight for the Fatherland."

"My name is Lieutenant Mueller. This case is pending. I'm tailing this young Austrian. He is friendly with a prominent citizen in Munich. That also could be a problem. He also cavorts with a known convict named Grab."

Mueller held up a big satchel.

"As for my other cases—a Russian doctor may try to enter the armed forces of this country in order to spread Marxist subversion . . ."

Lieutenant Mueller, opening his satchel, pawed through the papers of the other suspects with the corporal, taking notes again on his little pad.

"I always get my man, Corporal," said the Lieutenant gravely.

"What do you think of my new apartment, Audi? It took ages to talk papa into allowing me to have it," said Francesca with her voice laden with excitement. "After all, this week I turn twenty-one."

Audi saw that Francesca wore a sheer dress of pink cotton, belted at the waist with black satin. She had on one of those newfangled scarves wrapped around her head, with some type of Egyptian design printed on it.

"Your apartment is quite pleasing to the eye, Fraulein Francesca. I am not much for modernist styling, but this is quite nice," he commented in a guttural, Low German accent.

Audi wasn't sure about her strange clothes, questioning the modesty and demeanor in the young woman. "Independence may not agree with you after all, my dearest Miss."

He sat on her white leather couch with his little package in is hands. He held it up to her, and then put it down on the couch beside him.

"It's a birthday gift. I guess it's a housewarming gift too. The money from my two sketches came in."

"How nice of you! But first, I have something for *you*, dearest Audi."

"What are you doing over there, Fraulein?"

"The name is *Francesca*!"

"You've had your head buried in that closet for the last five minutes."

"I'm unpacking my stuff to find your gift. I have some nice wine from the Mosel Valley, too."

Francesca, who had just greeted him at the door minutes before, ushered him in to take a seat while she fetched a package from her cluttered storage across the living room. As she did so, Audi glanced around.

Located on the *Schellingstrasse*, her little, one bedroom apartment looked bright, modern, and cozy.

There were contrasting, pastel colors. Blond pine furniture and art deco fixtures—a style just emerging with the smart set—dotted the interior. With the exception of one item, thought Audi, her wall decorations were unusual but of acceptable taste. He realized that he was unused to such high tone flummery, but he felt himself nevertheless to be an expert on proper German taste.

Audi then noticed a medicine bottle sitting on her end table. Then, he remembered her little spell of shortness of breath soon after he had first met her.

Francesca walked toward Audi with her package in one outstretched hand and a bottle of white wine in the other. A corkscrew and two wine glasses already sat on the triangular, silver and glass coffee table in front of him.

Audi tapped his foot nervously as he watched her approach, not used to being alone with attractive young women anywhere, let alone in their stylish apartments. "For me, Fraulein?"

"For you, my *savior*," she said as she handed him the plain box. "Sorry I didn't have time to wrap it."

He laid it on his lap.

Her radiant eyes studied him closely as she put the bottle of wine down on the table next to the glasses and opener. She turned on some music that played on one of those new, expensive phonograph machines imported from America.

To Audi, the music had a strange, rhythmic quality. It possessed a strong beat similar to that which he had heard in the circus in an African exhibit, only with lots of low and then high tones from brass instruments. He thought he heard trumpets mixed with the other noise.

"It's called '*jass*', or something like that," she offered, noting the crinkling of his nose. "It's the latest thing. You don't like it, do you?"

He said nothing, not altogether pleased with her choice. She smiled, sitting down on the couch close beside him, her hips just touching his. He reflexively scooted away from her a bit.

"I had no trouble finding your place," he said without looking at her. "Fortunately, it's located next to my favorite restaurant—The Shellingstrasse Salon." In fact, Audi had stopped going there since the owner had refused to run even his small tabs.

There was a pause.

He coughed nervously. "I can assure you, Fraulein, that I am unaccustomed to visiting young women—"

"—I know, dearest Audi, that's why I find you so charming."

He eyed the package Francesca had given him.

"Open it," she commanded.

He unwrapped it, and then held the small painting up to the light. It shinned through the nearby window, soft and cloud-filtered.

"Fraulein Francesca!"

In Audi's hands presented a small reproduction of one of Rudolf von Alt's early pieces, *Stephansdom*, circa 1832.

"It's only a copy, of course, but I thought you'd like it."

"Oh, I do, Fraulein Francesca! I do most assuredly."

Audi examined the geometric, almost scientific lines of the gothic spires of the cathedral, against the naturalistic tones of the blue sky.

"Wonderful! Much better than the monstrosity over there," he blurted as he nodded over toward another painting hanging on her wall.

"Sorry, Fraulein, I'm too honest."

"Not at all. I want us to be true to one another."

"Do not be offended, Fraulein, but isn't that twisted young man in the painting Vincent Van Gogh?"

"—Yes, his *Self-Portrait with Straw Hat*—and I love it."

Audi scooted a bit farther away from Francesca, turning his legs the opposite direction from her. As he spoke, he was seated in a way that made it awkward for their eyes to meet. "They say impressionists are physiologically sick people who can't see nature's true colors and shapes."

Francesca opened the bottle of wine. She poured two glasses, one short and one very tall—hers the tall one. She gulped it down quick, smiling as she pushed his glass toward him.

She quickly changed the subject. "What did you get *me*, Audi?"

He handed her the box.

"I already gave you a few of my sketches. This gift is a little more personal, Fraulein."

She opened the box.

"Oh my, it's beautiful, Audie!" She held the silver necklace up to the light. "I've never seen anything like it. What an arresting design."

"Do you really like it, Francesca?"

Audi looked on as Francesca studied the bauble that she held in her hand.

He had seen one like it in a museum of runic and Germanic art, a few years back. He felt that its twisted shape imparted great energy and feeling, so he had paid rather too much for it in the antique store.

"I'll put it on right now." She filled her glass and took a long draught. "Audi, you're not drinking."

She pulled her loose blouse down from her neck, unbuttoning it a little more.

Audi's eyes shot in that direction.

She clasped the necklace around her neck. "I shall treasure it always." She turned toward him on the couch, leaned over, and pecked a kiss on his pursed lips.

The shiny pendant dangled from her smooth neck as the top of her yellow bra showed.

Audi just sat straight on the couch, looking forward and at her, and turning red.

"Oh Audi, your blushing! You are so prim and shy—and *sensitive and gentle*. How charming!"

Audi slowly moved his hand to his wine glass, grasping it off the table as if a thousand volts of electricity might go through his arm at any moment. "I am unused to wine, dearest Francesca."

She stood up. "Just one glass."

"But, I must be in control of myself."

"Fiddlesticks!" She slurred the word. "I have to go pee."

She staggered over to the window and drew the curtain, and then over to the water closet across the room, shutting the door behind her.

Audi saw that there was a marked sway in her gait.

Audi, a bit alarmed at such stark language from his hostess about "having to pee," took a draw on his wine. He did it again. He felt nervous, and the yellow liquid tasted like vinegar, but not too bad.

Soon, his head felt lighter—he even heard a light buzzing sound. It relaxed him, and for the first time he noticed the lingering scent of Francesca's fruity perfume.

The strange music still played in the background, its infectious melody blending with the alcohol and the mood set by the dimmer lighting. He preferred his marching music to this jungle noise. Of course, either couldn't match his precious Wagner.

Audi lost himself in a brown study. He thought of Francesca, and what kind of wife she might make him. He thought of the corporal and what he had said about finding a nice German girl . . .

Francesca seemed headstrong and "modern"—qualities he found alien to his understanding of women. His mother had been the opposite, and he felt more comfortable with that. Still, Fraulein Schmidt had the Nordic beauty and presence he admired, and the citizenship papers he needed . . .

"What do you think, Audi?"

Audi gasped.

He felt the blood rush from his legs as a large wad of cotton formed in this throat.

Francesca stood before him, nude from the waist up, except for her white silk panties. Her skin glowed with youthful suppleness, her breasts protruding firm and erect.

The full but toned thighs, long and smooth, flushed with apricot tones except for the soft sprinkle of golden peach fuzz powdering her inner thigh—complimenting her long, golden curls.

She giggled as she put down her glass of wine. "Would you like to sketch me, Audi? I have some pencils." She laughed—to Audi—very wickedly.

Audi's eyes swelled, but nothing else did.

She put down her empty glass.

Then, she got down on her knees, between the coffee table and the sofa, leaning forward, unbuttoning his ghastly overcoat.

"I'm getting you some new clothes."

He could feel her breasts press against his knees.

Audi grabbed a pillow quick, jumping up from the sofa. His panic amused her.

"Here, cover yourself, my child!" He stooped over her, pushing the pillow against her bare breasts. "I respect you too much for this, Fraulein Schmitt!" He was flummoxed—and a bit angry.

How could his future wife act like this? He had expected his special *liebling* to be bubbly, plump, meek, and submissive. This headstrong and educated girl of the leisure class threatened him, he thought. He felt a panicky loss of control.

Besides, what if nothing happens?

Yet, Audi was drawn to her almost "masculine," animal magnetism.

How strange . . .

"Fraulein, the hour is late, and I must take my leave. The wine made me dizzy. Until the next time then—"

In a flash, Audi was out the door with his overcoat wide open, and without his painting.

Francesca shook her head and giggled. She plopped down on the sofa, fumbling with her odd new necklace as she poured herself another glass of wine.

As Audi tripped down the stairs that led from outside his *fraulein's* front door to the street, Lieutenant Mueller's eyes—magnified by his thick eyeglasses—trailed the young Austrian leaving her apartment.

He grinned with self-satisfaction as he scribbled in his note pad.

Audi stroked with his brush, standing before Herr Schmidt's three-story, neoclassical home, painting the ornate structure in watercolor at his easel. His commission had started a couple of weeks before, and he had progressed rapidly.

Francesca's father had largely ignored him during the process, never even inviting him inside the house for as much as a cup of tea. The young artist had also seen a forcefully built, middle-aged man come and go from the house, a real dandy with a huge walrus mustache, who at times glared at him with hostile, brown eyes.

He felt a bit of rage well up within him at the thought of such snobbery from these undeserving relics of bourgeois elitism. After all, he thought, we are all Germans.

Audi had questioned young Francesca about the pompous man with the walrus mustache, and she would divulge nothing. He had nevertheless noted the terror in her eyes at the mention of him.

In fact, he thought, that man with the Kaiser mustache was in the house *now*.

He is visiting his close friend, Herr Schmidt.

Francesca, who had quarreled with her father, rarely visited her home anymore, apparently satisfied with her new apartment and modern, independent lifestyle.

She had invited Audi over for frequent dance lessons since her birthday. However, he had been a hopeless pupil—clumsy and totally devoid of rhythm . . .

Audi felt too warm. The late spring had given way to a sultry, early summer. The trees lining the wide, cobblestone street showed their late blossoms and leafy, green plumes in the bright noon sun.

Audi, perspiring under his thick, woolen tunic, moist with paint and sweat, unbuttoned his wing collar and loosed the suspenders on his Bavarian *lederhosen*.

He glanced over at the house as he put his paints away in his case. The young artist, admiring his work, noted that his strokes with the paint brush had carefully—even scientifically—reproduced the contours and details of the magnificent home faithfully—if, it might be said by some—with little insight.

Nevertheless, the effort pleased him, and he had finished his job.

Greta, the maid, came out of the house and strode up to the earnest Austrian, her face taught with apprehension. "Excuse me, sir, but His Honor requests your presence in his study. You may leave the painting out here . . ."

Herr Schmidt didn't mince words.

"Take a seat, young man," his gritty voice commanded as he pointed to the sofa. His dark business suit gave him the look of an aggressive prosecutor. "I must inform you of a few important facts."

As Audi entered the study, the stern expression of Francesca's father greeted him like a slap in the face. His tight fist clenched his pipe as he stood stiffly behind his desk.

Audi, showing no emotion, sat down calmly.

He glanced at the other man in the room. The pompous, middle-aged man with the walrus mustache had planted himself on the other side of Schmidt's desk, his savage, bull-like eyes poking into Audi's eyes like hot needles.

"This gentleman is Professor Zimmerman. He is Francesca's *fiancé*," said Schmidt gravely as he waved at his friend.

Both men locked onto Audi's reaction to that introduction. Audi's expression didn't change.

The walrus mustache stood arrogantly, one hand on his hip pushing back the coat of his expensive, brown-tweed coat, the other resting upon the corner of Herr Schmidt's desk.

"I understand your name is *Audi*," he blurted with palpable distaste, as if mentioning the name of an unmentionable product of digestion.

"Yes."

"Herr Schmidt and I have information that you have visited the rooms of his daughter—at unsuitable hours—in an inebriated state. You are offering gifts of a *personal* nature."

Herr Schmidt chimed in. "We also know that you associate with known hooligans, one a convicted felon—"

"—Then there is the issue of *your* criminal record, Herr—I really *don't know* what your family name is—*sir*," shot Zimmerman as he pulled a little bag out of his tweed coat.

"You told Schmidt here that you attended the Vienna School of Architecture. I know that you were rejected! We also know that you are running from the law!"

Audi slowly stood up from the sofa. His eyes gleamed like blue daggers as he glared from Herr Schmidt to Professor Zimmerman, remaining silent as he defiantly folded his arms.

"Here are your fifty marks for your commission," rattled Zimmerman, his middle teeth showing below his mustache like fangs on a snake. "With an *extra* fifty for coming to Francesca's assistance in May—when she was accosted while she walked in your seedy neighborhood."

He threw the bag of coins onto the sofa next to Audi. "You may take your painting of the house with you, sir."

Audi marched up to Herr Schmidt.

"Herr Schmidt. There are two possibilities. Either your friend is a lunatic, or he is a scoundrel. You may choose."

Audi turned on Zimmerman.

"I do not cavort with hooligans, Herr Professor. My men are honest toilers, patriots, and *Germans*!"

Audi bent over, sweeping the bag of money from the sofa onto the floor. "The money is now low enough for even you, Professor Zimmerman."

He strode to the door. "No one shall be allowed to bully poor Francesca. She's not your painted poodle. She is a celestial maiden, a handmaiden of destiny!"

Schmidt and Zimmerman looked at each other, lost for words. Audi barged out the study. As he did so, Zimmerman rushed after him, heading him off at the opened front door. He moved close to the proud young Austrian, face to face.

Zimmerman reached into his coat pocket.

Audi looked down. His eyes caught the gleam of a derringer pistol pointing at his heart.

"This is for you, Audi, if you, or *any* man, comes between me and Francesca. She's done with her *slumming*, understand?"

Zimmerman's eyes widened as he examined the surprising expression in Audi's gaze—a distant, steely, ethereal starburst—with a blue chill that froze his opponent's very soul.

Audi smiled faintly. "You dare say that to *me*. I warn you, Herr Professor, I have one of those too."

Audi then spit right into Professor's face.

He continued out the door and down the tree-lined street, proudly taking his painting that he had left by the street with him.

Audi sketched in his tiny, flophouse studio from images on postcards pasted on the cracked and moldy drywall behind his messy, single bed. Dark and cramped, and with no windows, the heat of the noon hour on this humid, mid-summer day stifled him.

He sat alone at his stool, moving his soft pencil over the easel, the marks taking form as Munich's famed *Hofbrauhaus*. His baggy overalls overflowed with erasures and pencils as he toiled in the light of a flickering candle, electricity being too expensive for this home of the down-and-out.

A rap at the door, and Goldfarb entered puffing one of his long, stem-handled cigarettes. His tall, lean figure—filling a trim, cutaway morning coat with a high-buttoned waistcoat and creased, fly-front trousers—hovered behind his Austrian protégé as he sat drawing. The salesman's quick, dark eyes appraised the value emerging from his associate's sketching hand.

"I need ten more of those sketches, and fast," said the visitor.

Audi kept sketching as he shook his head, his eyes not leaving his easel. "Goldfarb! I already gave you twenty this week."

"No, fifteen."

"OK, fifteen—so then?"

"I need more."

"When I went in with you, we agreed on a certain number for me to do."

"Yes, but we had to drop the price to two marks so we could sell them. I told you. We need more to sell. Our revenue is down. If you want to make ends meet, we need more products."

Audi threw down his pencil. He grabbed an eraser out of his pocket. "I can't do any more." He erased a smudge on the easel.

"Then, you need to sketch just for me, Audi—and only sketches. I must have all you do. Otherwise, we need a new gig."

Goldfarb looked around him, loosening his collar. "Boy, it's hot in here. Why no windows?"

"My digs aren't as fancy as yours, Goldfarb. Neither are my clothes," said Audi as he inspected his associate's fancy duds from head to toe.

"Surely, Audi, you have something."

Audi sprung up from his stool. He strode over to his little closet and threw it open. Some paintings and boxes fell out on the floor.

"Look through those. I think some sketches are in there."

Audi sat down again and started a new sketch. "Go ahead, take a look."

The sales agent moved over to the closet, rummaging though the wares. He pulled out a half-dozen squares of art—old sketches of Munich's Grand Opera House.

"These will do, Audi. I'll just take two for now."

Audi worked busily without paying Goldfarb much mind. He said nothing.

"How many—*exactly*—do you have of these, Audi?"

Audi broke his concentration.

"What? How should I know? Go ahead, I'm working!"

His agent put the sketches under his arm and headed for the door.

"You should really keep better inventory, Audi. I'm trying hard to sell your stuff, my friend, and it isn't easy."

Audi looked up from his easel, his eyes narrowing with irritation.

"Not easy? What do you mean? These are pure works of art. They speak to the heart."

"Right," continued Goldfarb, "the market's flooded. There's talk of war and people are hoarding their money. I had to buy a dozen of your pieces last month at half price, and now I'm stuck with them."

"All right!"

"It's getting late, Audi."

Goldfarb took another puff and left. He closed the door behind him hard.

Audi waved the residual smoke away.

"And don't smoke in my bedroom again, you hear Goldfarb!"

Audi realized that his career as an artist—even an artist of architecture—was melting. What was left, he lamented?

What is my true purpose in life?

Disgusted, he jumped up from his stool and then kicked over his easel, smashing it to bits as he stomped it into the dirty floor.

Audi roamed the streets on the sultry evening. It was too hot to sleep. His mind raced.

It seemed that the world was closing in on him. He had nothing but problems.

His Francesca was being corrupted by a world she scarcely knew. How *could she* know it?

She was but a child, he thought, and didn't know her mind. She was really an exalted angel, not the loose and modern city girl that she pretended to be. He knew she had virtue, and he wanted to make her his queen.

I must protect her purity!

His host country, his dream, was symbolized in her virtue. This was his wonderful land of coo-coo clocks, Goethe, clean alpine forests, deep mountain lakes, strudel, Wagner, the Brothers Grimm, and noble Siegfried and Brunnhilde.

They had continued seeing each other, but Audi, nevertheless, had doubts about her. He emerged from his reverie across the park from Francesca's apartment.

He needed his spirits lifted, having received terrible news that very afternoon. Audi removed a telegram from his shirt pocket and read the first sentence yet one more time:

"The crown prince regrets to inform the applicant that the petition to join the list regiment is herby denied . . ."

Audi knew this meant that his best chance to gain German citizenship was now to marry dear Francesca. He would then fulfill his life's dream and become a proper German—and then a citizen who, if war came, could enlist.

Standing across the park from her apartment, he could see her front door, knowing that any moment his true love might walk out . . .

Then, he wiped his eyes, trying to make out the dark figure slipping out from the entrance.

At this evening hour, out crept a strange creature from the door of Francesca's apartment.

A dark-bearded, foreign-looking, middle-aged man, wearing a fancy suit, closed Francesca's front door quietly behind him and left.

Could this be one of her eccentric uncles that she had told him about?

Who could this strange man be? Is it possible that she is—? No, this woman may become my wife!

Audi also knew that within three days he would be deported back to Austria.

Audi, depressed and sleepless after a night of tossing and turning, jumped out of bed, throwing on his filthy *lederhosen* and alpine shoes.

He opened the closet door to get his sketches, counting each one. Counting only three instead of five, he flew into a rage—throwing the sketches back into his closet.

"What on earth—?" he growled to himself. *Have I been cheated?*

He raced down the stairs, hoping that he may catch the last of the soup just before the time lunch would end. On the way down, he met Goldfarb coming up the stairs.

"Goldfarb! I must talk to you!"

Goldfarb stopped on the step below Audi, folding his arms.

"I have to talk to *you*."

"Oh, is that so?"

"I'm sorry. We have to call it quits, Audi. Nothing is selling."

"What do you mean?"

"Your sketches don't sell. I can't afford to buy them any more at half price—at *any* price. I can't sell them."

"Nonsense! You're a liar."

Goldfarb's eyes flashed. "We're even! Nothing is left. I'll just keep the sketches I have, and hope to sell them in the future."

He shrugged, turning to go back down the stairs. "I'll see you around, Audi."

Audi moved down one more step, face to face with his agent. He planted his hands on his hips, his voice louder and with steel tones.

"We are *not* even, sir! You have at least two of my sketches that are *not* accounted for! You *owe* me for those."

Goldfarb took his hands out of his suspenders.

"Nonsense, Audi. I don't owe you a penny. If fact, I'm stuck with lots stuff I'll probably never unload."

Audi's eyes blazed. "'*Stuff*!'" The veins stood out in his neck. "How dare you? You insult *and* cheat me!"

Goldfarb walked down the stairs and out of the flophouse as Audi shouted after him.

"I shall get a lawyer!"

Wiping his sweaty forehead with his sleeve, Audi ambled down to the courtyard, it being deserted except for Grab.

The late-July heat made the big, bald man sweat clear through his dirty shirt, as he sat finishing his crust of bread at a center table. He looked up at Audi as his distraught friend approached.

Audi noticed the huge, red, iron-cross tattoo on the wrestler's massive forearm, a detail he admired.

"What's wrong, Audi?"

Audi plopped down next to the hulk. His head hung low. "I have two days until I am deported. The Crown Prince turned down my petition to join the army. There is no way I can serve my Fatherland. There is no way I can become a German citizen. I *refuse* to fight for Austria."

"Did you hear that Austria gave Serbia an ultimatum? Russia may mobilize, too, to defend Serbia," said Grab.

"My Francesca! What am I to do? How can I marry her after *this*?"

"What did she do to disappoint you so, Audi?"

Audi buried his face in his hands. "Oh, some strange man left her apartment—during the evening."

"A tart she is," grumped the old fighter.

Audi's face turned red. "No! There must be some explanation." His hands shook, his eyes blazed. "You take that back, Grab. This instant! She is above us all!"

Grab, rattled, put his hands up. "I'm sorry."

"She's my Francesca!"

"Pardon me, dear comrade. I'll make it up to you, dear Audi."

Still, Audi had his doubts.

Marriage—that was something that he had never entirely counted upon. He had his destiny to fulfill first, after all. And now, there was the revolting thought of this bearded foreigner he had to contend with.

"Her father hates me," explained Audi. "He wants her to marry some rich professor instead. Not only that, I must be careful. Her father is a friend of the police captain. What am I to do?"

Audi's eyes took on a hint of terror. "They could nab me—deport me any day back to Vienna! They may put me in an Austrian prison. Perhaps, I may go into hiding. Those scoundrels!"

"Speaking of scoundrels—" Grab looked over at the stairwell entrance across the courtyard. He held his nose. "—I saw Goldfarb going up the stairs toward your room."

Audi jumped up from his chair. "I just spoke to him. The swine cheated me. The last outrage!"

Grab looked up at Audi, his face a mask of fury. "What?"

"He stole my sketches!" Audi put his hand on Grab's massive shoulder. "What is this world coming to?"

Grab shook his head. In his anger, he reflexively bent the spoon in his massive hand. "Don't worry about him," spat Grab. "It's time that his kind learned a lesson."

Tears welled up in Audi's eyes. " . . . I feel low. Sometimes—I think maybe I should end it all."

Part Three:

"—SOMETHING VERY URGENT TO ASK YOU. MEET ME AT THE MUNICH COURTHOUSE STEPS AT 3 PM TODAY—AUGUST 2—"

The sun's rays just broke over the trees in the park and shined on the front door of Francesca's apartment.

Audi took the note for her in his hands and sealed it in an envelope, dropping it though the post drop beside her door. His eyes darting around to see if anyone could be watching him, then he quickly left.

Presently, the door opened and out walked the dark-bearded, foreign-looking man, buttoning his collar and straightening his tie as he carefully looked around him. He held a door-key, which he placed under the doormat, and left.

He carried with him a black bag, similar to those used to store overnight clothes. The stranger dashed off, passing the tree-lined park across the street.

Within the park, behind a tree, stood Zimmerman, his jaw set, his eyes blazing with fury as he spied on the entrance to his dear Francesca's apartment.

The professor's hands shook with rage as she reached into his coat pocket and fondled his derringer pistol . . .

"Where is he? Where is the foreigner that calls himself '*Audi*?' Tell me Matron, or I shall be harsh with you!"

The slim, grey-haired woman put her hands to her mouth, her fingers trembling. "I'm sure I don't know, Lieutenant Mueller. He is just gone, that's all. His clothes are gone too—and his sketches and books."

Mueller's buggy eyes, obscured by the film of dust on his thick eyeglasses, darted around the dark hobble, the lodging looking even more inhospitable in the dim light of the flickering candle. "Whose calling card is that over on the little table there?"

The distraught woman glanced at it. "I'm sure I don't know, sir. There's usually only one visitor that I have seen up here in his room—and that is Herr Goldfarb."

Mueller marched over to the table and picked up the square piece of paper. Pushing back his white fedora hat with the dark band, he read it to himself.

"'Goldfarb and Associates, Art and Furniture, Munich, Germany.'"

Mueller put it in his pocket. "We're looking for this young criminal from Austria. If you hear anything, Matron, make sure you contact us. He's to be deported today."

Odeon's Square crackled with revelry. Boys hung from poles, young men in fine suits marched in sloppy formation down the street carrying their rifles, and young women lined the street, cheering them on, waving their handkerchiefs and tossing garlands before the parading volunteers.

A huge banner hung in front of the *Feldherrnhalle* Monument.

"GERMANY DECLARES WAR ON RUSSIA! GOD'S SPEED TO OUR TROOPS! DEMONSTRATION FOR THE WAR HERE AT 4 PM"

Goldfarb ambled down the deserted alley past the news kiosk. Most everyone was reveling in the public squares and main streets, leaving much of the city deserted, including the back alleyways. He had just come from the flophouse, trying to find Audi.

He had sold only one more of his client's residual sketches, and, out of kindness, he wanted to give him his meager share of the proceeds. But, Audi's landlady—who looked very nervous—had said that the young lodger had vanished.

The agent could hear the cheers of the crowds even from the alleyway, the city town folk going wild over the news of the war with Russia. As he just past the news kiosk on his way to Odeon's Square, he heard heavy steps behind him.

He spun around.

Grab's meaty face stared him in the eyes, his porcine glare burning with excitement. Goldfarb had just enough time to notice the ruffian's muscular forearm—and the red, iron cross tattoo—shoot towards his face.

The ruffian's brass knuckles flashed in the noon sun. Goldfarb felt his jaw separate from his face.

Then his nose crunched and his teeth shattered, so fast that the impending loss of consciousness pre-empted his pain.

As the victim fell to the gravel, Grab kicked him in the ribs.

The huge brawler then stomped on his victim's face with the heel of his boot. He kicked him again and again and again in the gut, until the blood rivulets draining from his mouth onto the ground formed a red moat around his motionless body . . .

Lieutenant Mueller stood over Goldfarb's corpse. The poor young man's face resembled ground beef. He reached into the pocket of the victim's tailored, dark suit—and noticed the stem-handled cigarettes that had spilled out onto the blood-soaked alley.

He pulled out a calling card and read it to the uniformed policeman standing next to him: "Goldfarb and Associates . . ."

Mueller then pulled out another card just like it from his pocket and held it up to the other card, realizing that they matched identically. He turned to his associate who was busy taking notes of the crime scene.

"This card connects a young Austrian with this victim. We've got to find this fugitive from justice, you understand?"

"Yes sir."

"I think I know who may give us his whereabouts."

"Who is that, sir?"

"Young Francesca Schmidt and her father. Fancy folks—we must tread lightly here, you understand Fritz?"

Fritz's shiny blond hair and neat rows of white teeth made him look more like a choir boy than a hardened cop. "Yes, sir, I understand the family is friendly with Captain von Braun."

"That's right, Fritz. I left word with Herr Schmidt that I'd like a word with him and his lovely young daughter. She's quite the little tart."

Mueller stood in Herr Schmidt's study with Francesca and her distraught father. His eyes darted between the two as they both sat silently on the sofa. He stood over them, taking notes on his pad as he gently plied his questions.

"You haven't seen this man named Audi for days then, is that right Fraulein?"

"Yes, Herr Lieutenant."

"Why? Were you two not sweethearts?"

Herr Schmidt jumped up from the sofa. "I beg your pardon! My daughter—"

Mueller put his hand up. "—Forgive me, Herr Schmidt, but I am only doing my job."

"We've been over this and everything else many times—" Herr Schmidt slowly sat back down, waving his hand for his daughter to answer, as if realizing that further resistance was foolish.

"—Well, yes and no, Lieutenant Mueller," said Francesca. "We weren't that close, actually. Audi hasn't been around much either the last few days, I don't know why. I *do* know that he and Professor Zimmerman had words. Zimmerman threatened Audi with a pistol—"

"Over you, Fraulein?"

" . . . Yes, I believe so."

"What kind of pistol, Fraulein?"

"A derringer, I think. He's insanely jealous."

"Fraulein, I hesitate to bring this up, but you have been meeting with another man besides Audi—a Frenchman, in fact. Have you not?"

"What's this?" interjected Herr Schmidt.

Francesca glanced at her father, sheepish look appearing on the face, "Yes Father, I never told you. In fact, we are secretly engaged. He's with the consulate."

Francesca blushed as Herr Schmidt's face contorted with anger. "A Frenchman too!"

"I see," said Lieutenant Mueller with a note of embarrassment, "does the name Goldfarb mean anything to you Fraulein?"

"Yes. Audi had a friend named Grab. Grab and Goldfarb didn't like each other."

Francesca looked at her father, then back at Mueller. "That's all I know, Lieutenant."

"Thank you, Miss. That's all for now. I'm sure you'll have the good sense to let us know if Audi contacts you."

"Audi was just here about two hours ago, Lieutenant Mueller. He is now a private in the Kaiser's List Regiment. He goes off for training first thing tomorrow morning, and then it's off to the front line!"

Mueller stood over the messy desk of Corporal Stein. The recruiting official's green eyes shinned with patriotic pride. "Any other questions, Lieutenant? I'm very busy. There's a war on now you know!"

Mueller put away his note pad, putting his hands in his overcoat pocket, trying to hold back his anger. "Yes, so I'm told. This man Audi is wanted in Austria. He's suspected—with an accomplice—of a brutal assault here on a man named Goldfarb. There's also a warrant for his deportation. Nobody's seen him except you, Corporal."

"Small potatoes—," shot Stein, "—compared to war."

"Not for Goldfarb."

"Like I said: 'small potatoes'."

"Where is Audi now?" shot back Mueller.

"How the hell should I know?"

The corporal shuffled his stack of papers. "Point in a drunken crowd; maybe that's him."

"Corporal Stein, I protest—"

Stein shot up from his chair.

"—Look here! We are in a fight for our lives with Russia. Soon, it will be France and England *together*. We don't want schoolboys. We *do* desperately want tough men that will fight!"

Just then, Mueller's clean-cut, blond subordinate—Fritz—strode into the office. His Prussian-blue policeman's uniform looked as clean and shiny as a freshly minted mark piece.

"Excuse me Lieutenant Mueller. A body of a man has been found—in the park across from Herr Schmidt's house."

Mueller frowned. "Who is he?"

"We don't know. But he has a dark beard and carries a black bag—he's about fifty."

The fresh young cop looked down at this notebook. "We think it's the Russian who has been frequenting young Fraulein Schmidt's apartment. He's known to be a Marxist, too."

Mueller thought for a moment. "Anything else, Fritz?"

"No, except someone put a bullet through his eye. The hole looks like it could have been from a derringer."

Mueller looked off into the distance, lost in thought.

"We'd better get over there fast."

"Audi, what's going on? Where have you been? The police barged into my father's house—questioning us about you."

Audi, looking around furtively, pulled Francesca aside behind one of the huge, ornate columns rising up from the steps of the courthouse's main entrance.

"Is it much past three o'clock?" continued Francesca, somewhat out of breath. "I hurried the best I could." She smiled at him.

He grabbed both her shoulders, pulling her close to him. "You must listen to me, Fraulein!"

His light blue eyes shot through her like one of those experimental x-ray machines.

"What's wrong?"

"Fraulein Francesca, before this morning, I was *forced* to marry you in order to stay in Germany. Now, that pressure is gone! Germany is at war, and they've inducted me into the Kaiser's Army. I'm officially *German* now! They even gave me a bounty for new clothes."

She stepped back from him, scanning his general appearance. "Audi, you were *forced*—to marry *me*?" She looked at him doubtfully, and then quickly changed the subject. "I must say you do look different in your new clothes."

He wore a cheap but clean, dark suit with a white dress shirt and dark tie. He had also grown a short mustache in the few days since she had last seen him.

"My time is short, Fraulein."

"When do you leave for the front lines? We simply *must* have a going-away party!"

She liked his mustache. It made him appear more *formidable,* his slightly receding chin being less noticeable. Audi seemed to be something of changeling, and his manner had taken on a strange new flavor.

She looked around her. "Why did you want to meet here? I got your note, of course. What do you have to tell me that's so important?"

"We're getting married! I shall still marry you, Fraulein, even though . . . perhaps, you are not pure. The fault is not all yours. I shall do you that favor."

Francesca's eyes flashed with indignation. She pushed him back.

"What? Not *pure*? A *favor*! Are you crazy? Besides, I never wanted to *marry* you! In fact, I'm already engaged, Audi—to a French gentleman—a man of distinction. I meant to tell you earlier."

Audi's face turned red. "Frenchman!"

He bit his lip so hard that a tiny trickle of blood oozed from his mouth. He wiped it quickly with his sleeve.

"Yes, you *did* want to marry me!"

"No!"

"Then, you led me on!"

He wiped his mouth again, the red color of his lips—with his savage blue eyes—making him look even more unhinged. "You did things that only a woman betrothed to a man would do."

"You misunderstood me."

"You're just *saying* that because *I* no longer really want *you*!"

"Nonsense!"

"You are *beneath* me, Fraulein!"

She started to walk away, but he grabbed her elbow, forcefully yanking her back.

"I know what it is. You share your bed with that old, *Russian* swine! I saw him leaving your place this morning! I'm not rich enough—"

"—You fool!"

He slapped her hard.

Francesca staggered back, dazed from the blow. The unmasked maniac confronting her unsettled her mind.

"I'm better than you are. You barracks whore!" She noted that his voice took on a gritty, guttural baseness that connected to an inner, violent core.

Francesca looked around her for help.

"I'm in the Kaiser's Army now, you hear? I don't need you or your stinking foreigners. How could you be a tart for that Russian?"

Her eyes blazed as she regained her confidence, and realized the fear of what Audi may be capable of.

"The '*Russian swine*' is my doctor!"

"Doctor? With your key and his overnight bag? I was there. I saw him. I was just leaving your apartment!"

Francesca's breath, with all the excitement, turned to respiratory stridor. "You've been spying on me?"

"Yes!"

She slapped him back, squarely across the face. For a moment, he was stunned.

"That's his . . . *doctor's* bag—not his overnight bag! I let him . . . have a key. He does house calls in emergencies—like my asthma attacks—you beast!"

Francesca started to feel faint for lack of air.

Audi grabbed her again.

She pushed him back again, harder, knocking him off balance. She looked around desperately for help.

Although there were plenty of people out, they were across the street, busy reveling. She didn't see any police. In all the noise, she figured, no one could hear her scream if he started to beat her.

Audi regained his footing, trembling with rage. "I'll bet he's a goddamned Jew!"

"A *Jew*, huh Audi? Well, *I'm* a goddamned Jew!"

Audi's jaw dropped.

"Yes, that's right, your dear sweetheart!"

Francesca, wearing the necklace over her blouse that he had given her weeks before, ripped it off and threw it in his face.

"My mother, God rest her soul, was raised Jewish, so technically . . . that makes *me* Jewish too! What . . . about it!"

She could feel that her voice was getting weaker. Despite her condition, she realized she'd have to make a run for it.

Audi's contorted mouth formed a foamy patch of spittle as he chocked on his words. "You *mischling*—half-breed! You *subhuman scum*!"

Francesca put her hands over her mouth. The realities now hit her like buckshot.

"Goldfarb! *You and your friend killed Goldfarb.* The police suspected you. It was *you* behind the murder, wasn't it?"

"Yes, yes, yes! I was there! The little swine stole my two opera house sketches, so—"

"—You maniac—you *gave* those two sketches to *me, remember*!"

She pointed her finger at him. In her growing excitement, her asthma caused her to wheeze. "And . . . it wasn't . . . Zimmerman . . . who killed my doctor—*you* did *that*, too, didn't you?"

He stood silently, his eyes demonic beacons.

She shook him by his lapels.

"Didn't you!"

"Yes, yes, yes—that too! Why not? I can do anything I like! I answer only to history. You are against me, like all the others!"

"Oh my God . . . you monster!"

He lunged at her.

With all her remaining strength—and all the courage she could summons—she kicked him hard in the balls.

He fell to the steps, grabbing his crotch, screaming at her: "Filthy bitch! Slut! Traitor!"

She sprinted away as fast as her legs would carrier her, wheezing and coughing, her asthma compounding the shock of her terrifying revelation.

Four o'clock on August 2, 1914, marked the start of the massive demonstration in Odeon's Square, supporting Germany's declaration of war with Russia.

Thousands of citizens had crowded into the space in front of the *Feldherrnhalle*, bearing witness to the testimonials of young men stating why they had signed up for military service for the Fatherland. One such young man was Audi.

Mueller had expected Audi to be there at the celebration. Sure enough, he was right.

His prey stood almost directly in front of him, the young man with the unruly, dark hair throwing up his hands, cheering wildly in the crowd in his dark suit just a few feet away.

Mueller, wearing his white fedora hat with a dark band, and thick eyeglasses, had indeed found his man after his frantic search—but now what?

The powers that be weren't too interested in pressing charges, even with the possibility of a double-homicide. The pesky Lieutenant had dutifully reported the crimes to Captain von Braun, and his subordinate Fritz had presented the evidence. They were in the square too, spying on the fugitive Audi, and any other young man who pledged that they would signed up—or would sign up—and then disappeared, shirking their responsibility to the Fatherland.

The captain, not sympathetic to Audi's victims, and being a great patriot, had preferred to sweep the incident under the rug. This would also please his dear friend Herr Schmidt, who wanted the young man to just vanish, and thus avoid more unpleasant questioning.

They had the perfect out—the new war with Russia. Audi had just pledged his enlistment in the army, and the next day would be gone—probably forever.

Mueller saw the skinny, bald captain standing not twenty yards away from him, behind the large lion statue in the square, with Fritz at this side . . .

Captain von Braun, eyeing the crowd carefully, preferred to discharge the duty of police surveillance personally, enjoying the historical celebration and fresh air. He had sported one of those newfangled portable cameras around his neck while stalking his prey. He was snapping photographs of the young men who lined up to give the enlistment testimonials.

He liked the clean cut and capable young police recruit next to him, who also scanned the noisy crowd in the square. To Captain von Braun's satisfaction, the young Austrian upstart happened to be there in the crowd too, standing just in front of their field man, Lieutenant Mueller.

"What's that in your hand, Fritz?" asked the captain, as he aimed his camera at the elated young fugitive cheering in the crowd—the one with the dark suit and mustache that had evaded Mueller for days.

The blond young policeman held up the silver bauble. "It's the necklace that Fraulein Schmidt threw at that young mam—who calls himself 'Audi'."

"The one that's over there in the crowd, in front of Lieutenant Mueller?"

"The same, sir" said Fritz. "The one that's suspected of the murder of the Russian doctor. He and his friend beat to death the peddler named Goldfarb. We found the necklace on the court steps just an hour ago."

"Odd looking piece of jewelry, isn't it?"

"Yes sir, quite different."

"Audi just joined up with the List Regiment, did he not?"

"Indeed he did, sir."

Von Braun considered. Through his camera lens, it seemed to him that this jubilant young man had just found his mission in life.

"Well then Fritz, let him beat Russians to death."

The roar of the revelers was deafening, so Fritz had to shout. He held up the silver necklace, staring at its odd, crooked form. It seemed to seduce him—the sun's late afternoon rays making it gleam.

"Do they have a name for that charm?" asked von Braun, somewhat taken with it too. "Speaking of names, what is the *real* name of this troublesome young Austrian chap? I just snapped his picture."

Fritz put the pendant back in his pocket.

"Some call the charm on the necklace a '*swastika*'. And that rascal over there is young Adolf Hitler. I guess we won't be hearing much from him anymore."

END

Novelette Three: A Cellist
Part One:

Tallulah Light-Hanford—or "Tully"— as her admiring public called the eccentric oil painter from Belfast, Ireland—stroked her easel with the rich, thick pigments, forming the outline—in bright white—of a slender man standing in a black background.

Her glowing, hazel eyes widened at the shock of this silhouette's predictive power.

The hand slightly withered, the bejewelled fingers a bit unsteady, the image had emerged from her painting fine and true nevertheless. She pushed back her white hair, pointing to the picture and speaking in her usual low-pitched voice.

"Don't look at me like that Harriet," her arresting stare targeted her young attendant standing beside her, "it just happens, that's all. The brush isn't under my control—you know that. It's rather like an Ouija board."

"Of course, Madame," Harriet responded in a grainy tone. Unlike her employer, she commanded a powerful, compact figure with a small chest and a decisive, matter-of-fact demeanour—not the tall, flowing, graceful lines of the famous eighty-year-old widow she tended to night and day.

Harriet's appraising brown eyes examined the image warily, "You'll meet *him* soon, ma'am." She repositioned the pearl comb in the thick, wavy, red hair that bunched atop her head. Her fine porcelain skin—somewhat incompatible with the plainness of her grey-muslin skirt and the white blouse with the stiff, high-necked collar—suggested refinement.

"Then, there's this one." Tully put down her paintbrush and turned her attention to the second easel standing beside the first one. "What do you think of it, Harriet? There's a sea with a horizon, but what is that dark thing?"

A soft violin—accompanying the golden tones of Caruso singing an aria—played from the funnelled speaker of the phonograph sitting on the credenza by the picture window. "Well? What does it remind you of?" asked the mistress of one of Ireland's finest mansions.

Two large, Chippendale couches and a desk sat open to the sweeping view from the sprawling Victorian home, the huge waves and turbulent sea crashing upon the rocks below.

Harriet's eyes shifted from the dark clouds outside the window to the second painting resting at chest level on the easel.

"Hard to say ma'am, looks to me like a ship."

The filtered light from the window lent the piece a particularly forbidding presence. "The dark object on the water," Harriet moved closer to the canvass, "could be a whale too."

Tully leaned toward the easel, examining her painting in minute detail: a sea of light blue, calm and still, with a long, dark, cigar-shaped figure on top of a flat line, stared her in the face. "Perhaps . . ."

"Would you be wanting anything else, Madame?"

"It's the sea, anyway," added Tully as she looked from the second painting to the gathering storm outside the window, "a calm one."

The old lady's eyes hardened. "It's the thirteenth anniversary coming up, isn't it?"

The women glanced knowingly at each other.

"My late husband's drowning, I mean Harriet."

"I know what you mean, ma'am."

Tully walked slowly over to the window, peering down to the crashing waves below. "He's down there somewhere—deep and dark," she whispered.

Harriet walked away from the easels and over to the desk, fussing with a mess of papers. "Are you all right, my lady?"

"Have Sam fetch the horse and buggy—I'm going down to the shore." Tully's eyes welled up.

"It's going to pour!"

Tully spun around from the widow, her glare aiming at the hapless body-servant. "Please do as I say, Harriet. Then, undress me—*completely*—except my heavy coat!"

Harriet looked at her employer warily. "Very well, as you say, Madame."

A tear rolled down the old woman's cheek.

"My fur hat too. Bring them *here*, please" she added as she started to remove her Delphos, finely pleated silk gown that flowed smoothly down to the rich, East-Indian rug.

"Let me help you with that." Harriet rushed over to assist her with the dress.

Tully stared out the widow, shaking. "There's something I must do. *Alone*."

As Harriet unbuttoned the gown, the handsome young maid's eyes flashed with apprehension.

Tully registered her attendant's expression.

"I'm not a crazy *spiritualist* like my critics charge! 'Ireland's *Certified Nut*,' the press squeals!"

"Indeed not." Harriet fiddled with the milk-glass beads on Tully's dress, suspended by silk cords along the side-seams, anchoring the gossamer, pastel material that hugged the surprisingly youthful lines her lady's graceful body.

"I'm just in touch with my soul, that's all," pleaded Tully as her voice softened.

At the crack of thunder Harriet jerked her head toward the window.

"Common sense," said Tully in a soft voice, "just a *different* sense, I should say." She glanced at her loyal attendant, smiling faintly. "Now run along dear, and do as I ask." She patted Harriet on her redoubtable shoulder.

Tully turned, glancing down at the raging sea once more . . .

"This good here, Miss Tully?"

"Fine, Sam."

Sam stopped the buggy carriage on the small beach next to the tall rocks, pulling hard on the reins. The old nags, sensing a storm coming, chomped at their bits, closing their huge, brown eyes to block the painful force of the gales.

"I'll just be around those rocks next to the water, Sam," said Tully, pointing in the direction of the breakers, as she held down her hat in the strong wind.

The driver, a skinny, ancient looking man with no hair or teeth, quickly buttoned up the collar of his long, thick coat. He jumped down from the buggy and helped his lady out of the carriage.

"Be careful, Miss."

Tully, wrapped in her wool coat and hat, made her way on the sand past the rocks, standing alone before the turbulent shoreline.

She peered into the waves, which pounded violently upon the dark, pebbly sand, hurting her bare feet. The deafening thuds of the crashing water assaulted her eardrums. The seaweed that had been washed ashore, mixed with the salt air, smelled very sweet.

Tully peeled off her hat. She dropped her coat to the ground, standing under the dark clouds without a stitch, the frigid air stinging her delicate skin.

She then ambled into the powerful waves.

The breakers pounded her body, but she caught herself, advancing deeper between the swells.

Presently, the short, grey hair disappeared under the seawater, and she was gone.

A huge wave then broke, carrying a large piece of light-coloured driftwood to the shoreline, depositing it upon the beach.

Only, it wasn't driftwood, but Tully, lying on the beach, coughing and thrashing as the water receded back into the depths of the savage ocean.

She slowly got to her feet and put her clothes back on, the horizontal-blowing sleet pelting her cold, wet body. She looked up at the sliver of sun breaking though the billowing clouds, and screamed.

"Joshua! It's not my time yet!"

"First Officer Hamilton, Madame. We'll be leaving Southampton directly. The porter here will direct you to your first class cabin on the starboard side." He took Tully's arm as the porter—standing at the summit of the gangplank loaded with heavy luggage— pointed the way to Harriet, who stood beside her.

Tully jerked her coat sleeve from Hamilton's grasp. "I'm all right! Don't fuss me young man."

Her eyes surveyed the huge, white steam-liner with the multiple decks, then glanced at Harriet moving slowly along the passageway in front of her, bound up in heavy wool in the this cold, early morning.

"Harriet, who are all those street people over there crowding down the steps? The ones with the wretched clothing and bulky packages."

The First Officer answered for her. "*Third class* passengers, Madame, carrying their belongings. Don't fret about their likes. They inhabit a separate part of the ship down below—"

Tully turned on him abruptly, "I'm not *fretting*, young man, just curious. Why do they need a separate gangplank? They're not lepers—"

As Tully's eyes shifted back to the first and second-class gangplank, her eyes widened at the sight that took her breath away. She froze in silence. Reaching out, she then yanked Harriet's arm as the other passengers passed, drawing her young maid aside.

"Look down the gangplank Harriet—the handsome young lad in the frock coat!"

Harriet surveyed the crowd of passengers coming up the gangplank. "Who?" She cupped her hands over her eyes to block the sun's horizontal rays. "Do you mean the slender one, the fair boy, standing next to the steward that's carrying the cello case?"

Tully removed her hat, wiping the sweat from her forehead. "Yes! The one with the flat-cap—the graceful one—his beautiful face is an angel's face! And so slight—the cello case is nearly as big as he is!"

Tully felt something take hold of her—a force that she couldn't deny. The pretty boy had *virtue*.

Just then, the steward dropped the cello case on the gangplank down below, its loud thud audible clear up to top deck where the women and First Officer Hamilton stood. Tully pointed to the strange young man, her excited eyes latching onto the rigid First Officer.

"Young man, who is that boy down there in the flat-cap, next to the cello case?"

Hamilton, his eyes narrowing in annoyance and a bit of puzzlement, gently waved Harriet and Tully along, trying to keep the gangplank clear for other arriving passengers. He reluctantly turned his head to search the crowd below.

"That's young Roger Beacons. He's in the ship's band. The lad is substituting for his brother— also a well-regarded musician—who suffered a sudden illness. For his eighteen years, Roger's quite the star. He sure caught the owner's eye."

Tully turned to look at Harriet, their eyes meeting. Harriet nodded back in understanding.

"Now, move along please Madame, we wouldn't want you to catch your death out here in this nippy air," coaxed the white-uniformed Hamilton. "We'll have a late breakfast in the Fern Room on A-deck in about an hour."

The women studied each other's thoughtful expressions, not hearing the officer's words.

Tully nodded, placing her hand on Harriet's shoulder. She cleared her throat. "I think . . . this beautiful boy . . . *pulls,* don't you my dear?"

"The first class salt pool has a crack in it? So, the *second class* here pool is ample," pronounced Tully in a self-satisfied tone.

She looked around the palm-strewn spa with the medicine balls lying on the floor next to the dumbbells.

"I understand, ma'am," intimated Harriet.

Tully smirked. "There's no sign of him yet."

She and Harriet dog-paddled their laps in the heated, six-foot, saltwater pool on the second class, D-level deck. "It's getting close to suppertime, I should think Harriet."

"We've been swimming most of the afternoon. Aren't you waterlogged yet, Ma'am?"

Tully paddled to the shallow end, resting on the steps. Harriet followed.

"Would you like a Turkish bath, Madame?" Harriet adjusted the strap on her thick, one-piece bathing suit whose plaid, red cap matched the wool material of the bulky outfit. She scratched her shoulder. "Doesn't your suit itch, ma'am?"

"I know he's coming, Harriet. All musicians love to swim—my husband did. It relaxes them."

"Just as you say."

Roger Beacons entered the spacious, dimly lit room in his long, white-cloth robe. Standing at the edge of the nearly deserted pool, and spotlighted by the electric lamp shining down from above him, he nodded to the women, displaying his straight white teeth and pursed, pink lips that formed a puckish smile.

He slowly peeled off his robe. Gracefully turning toward the peg on the wall, he hung it as Tully's hungry eyes devoured every inch of the lithe boy from top to bottom.

"Madame, *please!*" uttered Harriet under her breath, as her gaze swept back and forth between Tully and the angelic boy, whose charms her employer couldn't help but ogle.

Tully studiously catalogued the shocking allure: flawless, smooth white skin with a healthy glow; wavy, ginger-coloured hair neatly cut at medium length; a slight yet athletic body with a nicely rounded derriere; a V-shaped torso underlined by his scant, yellow, one-piece trunks; gently tapered and toned legs and arms; and a liveliness in his step that gave him a sense of fluidity and grace.

She awed at his large, smooth hands and the aquiline, patrician nose. He wore his art, she thought.

However—what obsessed her most—were his light brown eyes that were the colour of pale brandy, but far more intoxicating. They shone with a radiance that befitted his surname.

Breathless and drained, Tully sat there motionless and silent, summoning up the courage to address the young god, when—in a flash—he had disappeared as fast as he had entered.

"His eyes *glow*, Harriet," said the old woman as she closed her eyes, "just like . . ." She was too upset for more words.

"When your brother put in sick, the owner of this ship insisted upon hiring you! He not only likes cello, he also seems to have a *bass* fetish. You're supposed to be a *bassist* also—not just a cellist—so don't forget it!"

Band Leader John Potts, a burly, dark-bearded, bearish man of thirty who looked forty, had cornered Roger Beacons behind the music platform in the first class Cafe Paris.

The lithe young cellist huddled against the wall, much as a condemned man might before a firing squad. Shortly, the music trio would commence their after-dinner gig.

As the blue-uniformed Potts towered over Roger Beacons, the stale breath from his tirade gusted into the young mans tranquil face. "I was supposed to play that damned bass myself, but I foisted that task upon you instead. That unwieldy instrument is *beneath* me."

The fat man held his stomach for a moment, seemingly experiencing some peptic mishap. "You'd better live up to your inflated reputation, my little dandy!"

Potts looked around furtively at the arriving dinner guests in the dimly lit, dove-grey painted restaurant with the maroon accents, as if fearful of causing a scene.

"Yes, sir," responded Roger, his voice calm and even, his pale eyes twinkling.

Potts glanced at the instruments on the stage. "I see your cello's here. You forgot your double-bass instrument again! I called the steward to fetch it."

The grizzly tones of the bandleader clashed with the ornamental smile plastered upon his face. "They'll be no prima donnas here, my boy," he uttered under his heavy breath, "no favourites either!"

"Of course, sir."

The men in tuxes filtered in with their wives, the ladies sporting long, frilly dresses with sinuous, curving lines and lacy ruffles, elegant yet informal— the silky fabric resembling the colours of wilted spring-flowers. Then, the other young men of the band entered through the back door, all bedecked in the same dark blue, naval attire of the bandleader.

Potts' round, piggish eyes narrowed menacingly as he surveyed his young antagonist. "My God in heaven! Where did you find those clothes? Raffish I say!"

"Sorry, sir," responded Roger.

"What's that around your neck, my boy?"

"A scarf."

Roger complacently added in a subtle, energetic voice. "All the rage." He winked at Potts, which only caused a more heated exchange. There was a look in the bandleader's eye that he didn't quite fathom.

"We don't wear red scarves! Those are for the ladies, do you understand?"

Roger made an unsuccessful attempt to supress his grin.

"Damnation boy! Well, I guess there's no time for you to change," groused the bandleader as he inventoried, not without some relish, the boy from head to toe: the black, patent leather oxford shoes and spats; ankle-length, creased, black trousers with cuffs; a brushed leather, black tunic with wing collars; and the white Panama hat with a red band—matching the bright red scarf around the musician's long, graceful neck.

"Don't screw up, Beacons! In a few minutes the owner will be here—in *this* room. You can't miss him. He's the tall, slim fellow with the Captain—and sports a white tux with a red carnation."

Potts marched past the stage and took a seat in the back of the restaurant, away from the paying guests.

The two other musicians busily tuned their instruments—a piano a violin. Roger gracefully took a seat behind his huge cello.

His cello stood at the platform's centre, his slender hands barely covering the breadth of the strings. Taking the bow in his hand, he tested the tonal quality of his weighty instrument . . .

Mrs Lucien Smith—or Prudence Butts Smith, from Detroit, Michigan—heiress to the Butts Fertilizer fortune in the United States, took a seat at the circular, inlaid, walnut dinner table in the Cafe Paris, waiting for the musical performance. Her two children accompanied her—a lean, melancholy, teenage boy dressed in a navy suit—and a plump, feisty, blonde little girl outfitted in a frothy, pink-laced dress.

Prudence, her husband a landlubber, had chosen not to go on the cruise, instead tending to his business. Secretly, she had welcomed this respite, since her husband smoked his awful cigars and had acquired—or so she had suspected—an eye for the type of beautiful, young women that frequented luxury cruises.

As she sat in her plain but expensive outfit—a white, cashmere dress with a black sash and cape—she adjusted her curiously incongruent mink cap that had slid sideways upon her abundant nest of black, wavy hair. The waiter had provided tea, which she carefully sipped in the liner's red and white monogrammed china, while the kiddies chomped upon crackers and butter.

Her appraising, cool, blue eyes hunted the room when they skidded upon the alien sight of the feminine looking young man on the stage—the one with the outlandish red scarf and gauche hat. His dress, so different from the other musicians, accentuated the offense of his prissy features.

She thought that this must be a practical joke put on by the ship's owner—perhaps some sort of impish circus or carnival to provide a scurrilous diversion to the high-paying but bored patrons.

But no, this is just bad taste, she realized.

How dare they sponsor this, and in first class too! And, in front of my children!

She eyed the young, nubile musician, watching closely how suggestively he moved his pelvis on the stool, and the anarchic look in his eye! He was so young, yet so *sensual*.

She glanced at her young son with horror.

Her son stared at the young man too—in fact it seemed like everyone in the room was! She reached over and covered her son's eyes, then told him to take the seat at their table on the opposite side—facing away from the devilish musician.

The room was nearly full as the red-vested waiters served the fist course of baked oysters and sliced ham. A very tall man, in a white tux with a red carnation, then entered the restaurant with a shorter man, who sported a white beard and a white naval uniform.

A buzz permeated the room, and Prudence realized that the owner had accompanied the ship's Captain to their table near the stage. Prudence had heard that the notorious owner, although said to be a good businessman, was rumoured to be reckless and somewhat lacking in character.

Prudence's eyes widened as she observed two outlandish women dressed in some sort of oriental garb—brightly painted silk robes with high collars—strolling past her.

Following the waiter to the table next to hers, they dared to come to dinner in what was the latest fad—the oriental flummery of the decadent and *newly* rich.

My Lord, what is next?

She glanced sideways at them. Her lips pursed.

I can't believe my eyes.

The old woman with the short, grey, man-like hair and the severe looking young redhead actually held hands as they sat complacently at their table!

Although revolted by such behaviour, Prudence was also curious—if not sensing a pang of titillation. "Don't look around children—just eat your dinner! It's almost time to go," she snapped. Of course, she rationalized to herself *European women,* who lacked character, often held hands in public.

Suddenly, the band played *Brahms' Sonata No. 1 in E Minor.*

Roger moved his white-hair bow over the strings of his cello with grace, producing the angelic cords and tones that soothed and exalted his audience. The din of chatter and clanging of dishes soon went absolutely silent as the trio finished the lovely piece.

Tully's eyes fastened upon her young boy, seemingly caught in a trance-like spell as the exalted number concluded.

The steward then barged into the restaurant with his trolley, pulling the huge double bass instrument behind that was cocooned within its massive cedar case. He lugged it up upon the platform, and then set it up for Roger to play. Its bass case, lying empty, looked like a giant, wooden pear.

Potts, sitting at the back of the room, pushed away his bowl of soup, noting the embarrassing interruption. He then looked over at the owner and the captain.

The owner—the middle aged man in the white tux with red carnation— nodded to the captain, pointing to the newly arrived instrument with a hint of mirth on his face, seemingly unperturbed by the unnecessary intrusion. He pointed out the young boy in the funny hat, his eyes sparkling.

Tully watched closely, as Harriet started to chatter about how Roger had dressed. Tully just smiled. She studied Roger as though he was a magician and she was trying to find a clue to his uncanny talent.

Prudence dug into her ham and oysters, stuffing the salty contents into her pouty mouth. She wondered about the instrument in the strange, gargantuan case. Bigger than—although similar to— a cello, she had never seen one before.

Roger Beacons, having opened the case with the steward, had propped it up on its endpin—the instrument standing over six feet tall. He took a seat on his stool behind it.

He plucked the four strings of the deep, rich bass to get a sense of its pitch. He made a few adjustments at the machine head below the scroll, and then commenced his true solo.

The room went silent once more.

Bach Cello Suite No. 1, Prelude in Double Bass bewitched its listeners as the low, sultry tones gave way to lilting, then sad colours of low-pitched sounds that many in the audience wept to, stunned by its emotional honesty.

Prudence, not moved, just scowled at the audacious young exhibitionist, reaching for the bottle of champagne. She coaxed her children to eat faster. Out of the corner of her eye, since she dare not look at the creature directly, she caught the sight of Tully rising from her table when Roger's piece had finished.

Prudence observed the old woman in the oriental outfit clapping as she approached the stage. Mrs Smith wanted no more of what had been a trying evening in the vaunted Cafe Paris. She abruptly rose, taking her children by the hand, and marched out of the restaurant, scowling at the strange woman as she attempted to speak privately with the outlandish young boy on the musician's stage . . .

Tully had stopped at the platform, just below Roger, reaching up to grasp his hand. "You know my dear," said Tully as she looked up into his bewitching eyes, "your instrument *sings* to us, it doesn't just play."

Roger smiled at her warmly, taking her hand, and then kissing it. The other patrons in the restaurant observed this unusual spectacle with some astonishment, even in such a sophisticated, cosmopolitan crowd.

Tully looked over at the huge case wooden bass case. "My late husband was a violinist. His instrument sung too."

"We're going to play something different now, Madame. It's faster, looser—some call it '*jazz*'," said Roger in a soft tone.

"My goodness," blurted Tully, "your instrument case is as big as a boat! It must be hard for such a slight youth like you to handle such a big instrument."

Roger peered down into the old lady's glowing eyes. "You are a kind, gently lady," he said sweetly.

"Young man, I must tell you something else."

"Yes, ma'am?"

"It's something my husband also possessed."

"Yes?"

"You . . . *pull*."

"What do you mean?"

"You may find out in due course, young man."

Roger looked at Tully quizzically, who then returned to her seat beside Harriet.

He glanced at the other musicians, snapping his fingers. The trio broke into a quick, sensual rhythm as Roger moved his fluid body to the beat of the seductive music.

He winked at Tully, and then lost himself in the rapture of the jazz.

The audience, surprised at first, clapped to the beat.

All of the sudden, the stuffed shirts in the Cafe Paris rose from their tables, and trotted out to the tiny dance floor. Under the blue lights, they started to dance—fast—to the pounding rhythm. It was as if they found something within their latent DNA that tapped into the rapture of seductive movement . . .

Tully looked on, the excitement on her face palpable.

"Harriet. We must go. I must paint. The power has come over me."

Harriet looked at her lady, her expression grave. "Yes, Madame, as you say."

They abruptly left the room.

Part Two:

Tully stood in her cabin in front of her easel, her wet paintbrush in hand. Harriet stood at her side. Both women studied the image intently, and then looked at each other with grim expressions.

"It looks bad. Evil is upon us, Harriet."

"Yes ma'am."

"My God! Not again."

"Don't distress yourself too much."

"My art sings to me. But the song of what is to come is sad—violent!"

Harriet put her hand to her mouth, and then looked away. She took a seat on the plush, cranberry coloured upholstery of the Queen Anne style chair.

"Are you frightened, my dear," asked Tully in a gentle voice.

"No."

Harriet looked out the porthole and into the early morning sky. "Just tired, Madame."

Tully backed away from the painting and walked over to the large bed near the ocean-view balcony. She sat on their rich, quilted bedspread and studied the sacred objects resting on the bed-stand.

Tully's shrine stared her in the face: an old violin; a red scarf; and an old photo of a fair-haired youth holding his violin. She picked up the violin and fondled it, plucking its strings.

"Joshua my dear. It sang to you too, didn't it my dear? We should have heeded the warnings." Tully put down the instrument and then picked up the silk scarf, running it over her face as she looked at the photo.

"They'll be no mistakes this time, my dear Joshua."

Tully put down the scarf and walked back to her new painting, noting its dark theme. What she saw troubled her immensely.

Tully studied the faces in the blue, bubbling void, contorted eyes savage and in terror, arms and hands clawing and flailing in the desperate struggle to survive just one more moment.

"Captain, I'm simply appalled. Did you see that *woman* and her . . . *companion* . . . in the cafe? *They held hands.* The old one—the one they call 'Tully'—then had the gall to engage that pretty young boy—the cellist—in a private and *lurid* conversation! And the subversive outfit he wore—and that strange music at the end with the . . . *thumping* rhythm. My God!"

The ship's Captain stood on A-deck looking over the railing and into the North Atlantic's smooth surface. It was a very still sea—very unusual.

He turned his head to look at the squat, tightly bundled heiress, looking like a fat beaver in her thick furs and silly hat with the stuffed birds perched upon its crown.

He shook his head. *Oh boy, another one of these busybodies again.* First he had to coddle the pain-in-the-ass owner, and now it's this bull terrier.

I can hardly wait until retirement.

"Mrs Smith—"

"Prudence—"

"—*Prudence,* how do you know the conversation was 'lurid'?"

"Did you see them *touching*, and the way he moved his hips, the way his eyes sparkled in front of everyone, and the way she ogled him up and down—just like . . . hedonists! No shame, no shame . . ."

"You seemed to notice a lot, Madame—"

"—And in front of my precious children, no less."

"Mrs Smith, what would you have me do?"

"Captain, this is Saturday afternoon. We arrive at our destination Monday morning. I refuse to look at those two for the duration. Do you hear me? My husband is a friend of the owner—and if I have to—"

"—I'll make a note of it ma'am. We'll keep an eye out."

"Call me Prudence!"

"*Prudence.*"

"This is important, Captain. I hesitate to state this openly. But, I suspect an *unnatural tendency* here."

The Captain watched her as she waddled away in a huff. He looked down into the sea. There's nothing as restful and quiet as retirement, he thought wistfully.

"I was very happy when I received your note." Roger stood next to the scoring triangle on the first class shuffleboard deck, as Tully sent the puck gliding along the court for a nice score.

She looked up at the dapper young musician, attired in pure white, with tight cotton slacks and a wool sweater with a yellow trimmed, v-shaped neckline.

"I want to know what you meant when you said that I '*pull*'," asked Roger. "What do you mean by that?"

Harriet, who took her position with her paddle, glanced at Tully. "Should we tell him now, Madame?"

"No, we should *show* him."

Harriet looked at her doubtfully and then took her shot, sending the puck sliding way past the scoring area.

"See what you made me do, ma'am?" she said with an impish smile, a twinkle appearing in the eyes.

Roger looked back and forth between the women. "Show me what?" He laughed innocently, his white teeth gleaming against the background of the smooth, blue Atlantic.

To Tully, the handsome young boy looked deliciously preppy in his yellow flat-cap and sneakers, matching the yellow trim of his sweater. She leaned over and aimed another shot, her long paddle in hand.

"You know Roger, games, like life, are more about feeling than knowing. Knowing is limited, and momentary."

She pushed to aim her shot. The puck whizzed past Roger and landed in the triangle. "Feeling is unlimited, and lasting. It *guides* most of what we do."

Roger adjusted his cap down more over his eyes, blocking the bright sun's rays. "Yes, but what has that to do with *pulling*?"

"I'll tell you." She motioned to Harriet to take her turn. "Some of us are called 'spiritualists', but it's really sensing what you already know before you realize it—that there are deep feelings that you'd better heed—or . . ."

"Or what?"

"Take this shot, for example," she sent the puck down the court with a fast shove of her paddle, "I *feel* where the puck will end up—knowing has nothing to do with it."

"I'm sorry—"

"Some of us are better at shuffleboard than others."

"And myself?" asked Roger—getting Tully's drift.

"There are markers. You have a couple of them." Tully waved to Harriet. "Take your turn now, dear."

Harriet took her shot.

"Like what 'markers'?"

"Thirteen years ago—almost exactly—my dear husband drowned in a shipwreck. It was very famous. It was a huge steam-liner."

"I see ma'am. I'm sorry."

"No you don't see!"

Tully hung her head. "I didn't mean to snap at you, my dear. He was a musician like you. His eyes shone like yours. His instrument sang like yours. One day you will understand what it's saying to you."

"Yes?"

"Yes. And, he *pulled* too."

"So, I must learn to sense what I already know, *before* I know it?"

"Exactly?"

"How do I know I can?"

"Before, I said I'd *show* you."

"How?"

"Come to our cabin late tonight."

" . . . All right. I shall come."

"Alone—

"Yes, alone."

Just then, Prudence Smith passed by quickly, her children in tow. She glanced at Tully with a steaming scowl, and then disappeared around the corner.

Roger watched the woman pass, and then looked at Tully.

"Until then." He started to leave.

"And my dear—"

He paused. "Yes?"

"I want you to remember this and do not forget it."

"What?"

"Attend to your double bass—keep it in its case when you can."

Roger's face registered puzzlement. He shrugged and disappeared into the lovely afternoon sun.

"All right, pretty boy! I told you not to screw up. Now look what you did!"

Roger sat in the ship's conservatory on D-deck, tunning his double bass. All the crew's eight musicians practiced on their various instruments, the room a cacophony of tones. Bandleader Potts smoked his big cigar as she stood over Roger, who was seated on his stool, his arm around the neck of his huge string instrument.

"I don't understand Mr Potts. What did I do?"

"First, you wore your outlandish clothes, shocking an important first class passenger. Moreover, you played that wild musical number for which you had no authority!"

Potts blew the cigar smoke in the boy's face. "Then, you have an intimate conversation with an *elderly* woman—according to some—of a *questionable* nature. Last, you meet with the same widow on the *first class* deck, at a shuffleboard game. That is a violation of corporate policy!"

"Did the owner speak well of my playing the double bass?"

"Well, yes. You do a fine turn on your bass, I grant you."

"All right then."

"No, it's *not* all right! Did you per chance happen to make an appointment to meet the elderly woman in her first class cabin?"

"Who—"

"—Never mind! You're residing now in second class. You're no longer welcome in second class, and you will have no access to first class unless specifically invited on that deck! From now on, your cabin is in *steerage*—third class! Is that clear?"

Roger put down the bow of his instrument. He slumped in his stool. "Yes, sir."

"Tomorrow morning, you move your belongings!"

"Yes sir."

Potts blew another puff of smoke into Roger's face, and then marched out of the conservatory.

"Look at it, Madame. What is that? What is it telling us?"

Tully and Harriet stood in front of her easel. The paint dripped from Tully's brush, her hand trembling. The old woman looked at the cobalt blue lines of the figure on her painting, not sure of its meaning.

Her hand had been guided by the deep sense within her, moving the brush over the canvass, then dipping the paint and guiding her hand. The process had consumed her, almost like a trance.

She stared at the image of what was to come.

"Can a mountain be blue?" asked Harriet as her eyes ran over the strange shape. She stood there, like her employer, in her sheer nightgown, her hair mussed.

Tully examined the shades and tones of her new piece, the thickness of the impasto and the hidden meanings buried within its rich swirls giving her a chill.

"It's a blue mountain without trees."

"Miss, we've been holed up here for an entire day, ever since you went into one of your spells."

Harriet looked around their dark cabin, the electric lamps glowing dimly and the curtain pulled, dirty dishes and empty pots—left over from room-service—strewn upon the table.

"Yes, not the festive holiday you'd hoped for Harriet, not entirely anyway."

Harriet's eyes shifted to the other two easels placed before them in their tall stands, with the black covers over them. She nodded in its direction.

"These two took me all night."

"I didn't see them, ma'am. You must have completed these while I was asleep. You should have nudged me."

Tully looked over at the messy bed across the room, the light blue of the cabin's walls matching the milk-blue of the crumpled bedspread.

She glanced at the sign resting upon the coffee table next to it.

"TALLULAH LIGHT-HANFORD ART EXHIBIT SUNDAY MORNING AT 10 AM AFTER CHAPEL SERVICE—A-DECK LIBRARY NEAR THE FORWARD STAIRCASE."

"Harriet, I want you to include these two covered paintings in the art exhibit tomorrow morning when you set up. Put the paintings in the gold frames. The ship's company has put the rest is storage."

Harriet's intense brown eyes flashed surprise.

"You've never done this before."

"Done what?"

"Mix them with your business art."

" . . . I know. Do as I say."

"Yes, ma'am."

"Don't forget to put the notice of the show in the library tonight."

"By the way ma'am, I sent the invitation to young Roger for tonight—near midnight. I tipped the steward a good sum, instructing him not to blab it about."

"He must be *shown*, Harriet! Or, he won't *heed* me!"

"Perhaps, but are you sure it's *wise?*"

"No, I'm not sure of anything, Harriet. All I *do* know is that we've precious little time!"

"Yes, I can see that." Harriet pursed her full, sensuous lips. She studied the face of her lady. "Young Roger Beacons is in third class now. Prudence Smith—the heiress—has caused a row."

"That old wet hen! They lock those people in at night—like cattle! The poor young, beautiful boy."

"Indeed."

"Now, let us dress for dinner. Get this gown off me, dear Harriet."

The Crystal Lounge was said to be the most elegant affair in the floating world—a society ritual for the wealthy and the beautiful.

They sipped their tea, after-dinner liquors, and champagne, listening to the finest classical music money can buy. They waltzed on a pecan-wood dance floor to the string melodies of Shubert, Bach, Beethoven, and Mozart.

Painted in bright white with light-pink trim, overflowing with yellow flowers in silver vases at every turn, and ornamented with hundreds of glittering, crystal implements from dishes to chandeliers, it reeked of the in-your-face elegance of the gilded age.

Restricted of course to the first class passengers, the patrons were allowed to wear only shades of grey, or pure black, or pure white. The men sat complacently at their circular, glass tables in tuxes, and women in flowing, semi-backless gowns with huge frilly hats sold only in the ship's store—a business innovation imposed by the steam-liner's entrepreneurial owner.

Tully and Harriet had, after dinner, been seated near the lounge's entrance, and Prudence Smith—minus her children—had been seated—by the white-coated waiters—close to the string quintet. A sweeping view of the ocean enchanted through a huge picture window.

"There she is over there right now, the fat pucker butt." Tully glared at Prudence, the officious heiress attired in a white, round-brimmed hat nearly as big as she was. "The fertilizer queen scowled at us when we entered. I might add Harriet, that her table is much better situated than ours."

Tully's eyes then sparkled when they shifted to Roger tuning his cello on the musician's platform.

Harriet glanced about the crowded room, which smelled of gardenias, the background noise of chatter accented by the tones of the band plucking and tapping their instruments.

Roger sat behind his cello with his bow in his hand, accompanied by other four young men—all in white tuxes with black ties—playing one piano and three violins. The only splash of colour in the whole place was their bright red berets, and the red carnations sticking out of their coat lapels.

Harriet filled Tully's glass to the top with pink champagne, then filled hers and gulped it down. Tully drained her glass as she eyed Roger Beacons. She licked the residual, pungent liquid from her lips as she twirled her glass. "Roger looks divine, doesn't he?

Harriet studied the young man too. "Indeed he does, ma'am; Quite the fair young god."

Just then, the band broke into a waltz.

Tully tapped her feet to the golden melody of Strauss. She drained a second glass as her gaze hunted around, examining the other passengers, her attention settling upon the sight of a grey-haired man conversing with a very young woman two tables away.

The man took the girl's slender hand and pulled her to the dance floor, when other couples followed their example and joined the waltz. After three numbers, the band then played a violin solo.

The dance floor emptied. Tully finished her fifth glass, whereupon she stood—propping herself up using the back of her chair—and stared at Roger as he quietly conversed with the young pianist next to him.

"My heart is sixteen Harriet, imprisoned in this shrivelled up shell of an old hag."

As Harriet looked the other way, Tully ambled toward the band, swaying widely as she stepped, almost knocking a table over on the way. The room grew quieter as many patrons stared at her as she made her way to Roger Beacons.

Harriet, finally watching the old woman, sprung to her feet when Tully almost tripped. Too late to intervene gracefully, she just sat back down. Tully stepped onto the stage and stood over Roger, extending her withered hand to the tender young boy.

The violin stopped playing its plucky tune. Roger slowly stood up from his stool, smiling at his gutsy admirer, taking her hand in his and leading her to the dance floor. Tully waved at the violinist, and the young man commenced his playing again.

The couple waltzed together as they held each other close, their bodies joined. Roger, the same height as his partner, put his smooth cheek to her face. Tully then turned her head slightly, looking into his eyes as they glided about the room to the rhythm of the waltz.

Tully kissed Roger on the mouth. "*Joshua*, where have you been?" she asked in a sad voice.

Roger's eyes registered alarm, then pity.

Tully stopped dancing, putting her hands to her mouth. Regaining her composure—she left the dance floor.

Bandleader Potts, having been seated in the back of the room—his fat belly protruding under his grey waistcoat—shook with rage, glaring at the young boy in his band and mouthing obscenities at him under his breath.

Prudence Smith sprung up from her chair and intersected Tully just before the distraught old woman had reached her table. "This is outrageous behaviour for a woman your age."

Her huge hat slid down over her face, which she quickly shoved back into place.

"Enough you fish-eyed, sex-starved hornet!"

Prudence's mouth dropped to the floor. "I've never—"

Harriet rose to her feet and moved quickly to her employer's side.

Tully laughed. "—Pick up your chin, lady. You can't afford to lose any more."

"You're a devil! I'll have you thrown into steerage . . ." Her hat slid over her face again.

Tully took her maid's hand and led her away from the table, her defiant eyes still fixed upon the nosy heiress.

"There's an old lecher billionaire over there dancing with his sixteen-year-old wife! You don't seem to have any problem with that, Prudence!"

"Are you ready to go back to the cabin, Madame?" asked Harriet calmly.

Tully, with a mischievous grin, ogled Harriet up and down, furtively winking at her.

She shouted in a voice loud enough that her foe was sure to hear.

"Come on baby, it's bedtime!"

Prudence covered her mouth in shock.

Harriet grinned as she and Tully marched to the exit, arm in arm, past the line-up of stunned passengers.

An army of waiters rushed to Prudence Smith. She lay on the floor with the giant hat blanketing her freckled face, much like a shroud for the dead.

Prudence had fainted.

"It has to be him at this hour—it's the boy, Roger. He showed up!"

Harriet looked up to the clock, both hands pointing to twelve. She walked to the door of their cabin and swung the door wide open.

"Hello Roger."

He entered the cabin like a gust of fresh air, his mirthful eyes playing the two women like his cello, light and fanciful. Appearing quite the dandy, he wore a plaid-cloth cap over his neatly combed, lustrous hair, and a long sleeved shirt with a winged collar, tall brown boots with tweed breeches, and a Norfolk jacket. He smelled of lilac and lime.

"I see I'm underdressed," he said, as he looked his guests up and down, smiling.

The two women, dressed in bulky, white, red-monogramed robes supplied by the cruise-line, glanced at each other and grinned impishly.

Passing Harriet with a slight bow, he strolled over to Tully who was busy at her easel. He studied the image on her canvass.

The boy, if not shocked, was surprised. "It *does* look like me. Are my eyes really like that?"

"Yes—" Tully, her hands covered in paint, put down her brush and washed them in the basin of turpentine. "But, it's not you my boy, it's my . . . dear ex-husband."

She picked the painting off the easel and held it up in front of Roger. Tully, Harriet, and Roger stood together, looking at the close up image of Roger's face, the eyes dominating.

The mix of the brown and yellow pigments had reproduced the magic of them—the glowing energy—the sensuousness and yet the innocence too. They, like the ginger coloured hair, played with the golden light from the Tiffany lamp hanging overhead.

He peeled off his coat and threw it nonchalantly over the back of the chair. "You were going to *show* me something?" asked Roger in his sweet, smooth, self-assured voice, his hand placed on his hip and his back arched—his tight bottom creasing like a ripe peach.

Tully and Harriet exchanged glances.

"You must trust me Roger."

"I do."

Tully put down the painting.

"You have it. My husband had it. I have it too. It's a burden and a blessing, my son."

"I am yours to command. Lead on," he said softly with a twinkle in his eye.

"Harriet, bring the candles. Fetch the pail of water too." Tully took Roger by the hand, leading him to the bathroom.

She placed him in the ornate room, with red velvet wallpaper and gold-plated faucets, in front of a body length mirror. Harriet entered behind them carrying two tallow candles and the pail of water.

She placed them on the counter by the bathtub, and then lit the candles.

"Turn toward the mirror, Roger my dear."

He did so.

"Harriet, take that towel over there and wet it in the pail of water, and then stand by."

"Yes, Madame."

Harriet did so, and then approached Roger.

"Now Roger, stand perfectly still. Do you understand?"

"Yes."

"Harriet, if you please," said Tully softly.

Harriet approached the handsome boy, getting very close to him. Her hands shook as she slowly removed his cap.

Then, Tully looked on closely as Harriet stripped his clothing off--slowly removing his shirt, then his boots and socks, then his knickers, and then his undershirt.

"The rest too, ma'am?" Harriet asked in a cracking voice, her eyes running wildly over the young boy as she performed her duty.

The warm glow of the candle bathed his firm, young body—the smooth, radiant skin reflecting the soft, golden light like a shining star reflects the sun.

"The rest too, or the energy will be blocked."

She peeled off the briefs, and Roger stood there in calm repose, his perfect, chiselled body expressionless and noble, like Michelangelo's young David, as naked as a starfish.

"Well, so far *I'm* showing *you*, I guess," said Roger mirthfully, "I hope you're enjoying yourselves."

Harriet chuckled. "Very much so, actually, Master Roger, more than I had anticipated—but that's quite beside the point."

"Quiet Harriet. Now, wipe down the young man with the wet towel."

Harriet took the towel and ran it over his body, until every square inch was moist. It glistened even more in the candlelight.

"Harriet, wet it again, and keep it handy.
"Blow out the candles," instructed Tully.

Harriet blew them out, and the bathroom went pitch black.

"Now Roger, get closer to the mirror."

Roger did so.

Presently, a faint glow—a silhouetted halo—emerged from the outline of Roger's body, so subtle that it almost defied close examination.

"Do you see the light around your body, Roger?"

"By God I do, Madame," he answered slowly, his voice now grave and subdued.

"What is it? I've never noticed it before."

"Well, you've never stood close to a body mirror before, examining yourself in the dark, wet and completely nude, now have you?"

"Harriet, drop my robe."

Tully moved beside Roger, close to the mirror.

"Yes Madame." She unbuttoned Tully's robe, dropping it to the floor.

"Wet me."

Harriet applied the wet cloth as she had done to Roger.

"Do you see me, young Roger?" asked Tully.

Tully's irregular outline was rimmed in a faint light as well, not as radiant, but nevertheless definitely there.

"Yes, I do indeed."

"Now you Harriet, do the same. We can crowd here side by side."

Harriet removed her robe, and applied the wet towel. Her well-toned body showed no rim of light.

"You see," continued Tully, "normal people don't have one."

"What does it mean?" asked Roger again.

"Roger, now this is what is important," answered Tully. "Move closer to the mirror, until you barely touch. I shall do so as well."

The both moved in unison toward the mirror just a tad, its outline barely visible, until they barely touched it.

"Roger, do you feel it?" asked Tully.

"Why, why . . . yes, ma'am," responded Roger. "It feels like the mirror is *pulling* me toward it. I can barely tell, but I can feel it—no doubt!"

"You *pull,* Roger. I told you that I would *show* you—prove it to you, so I did!"

"Lord! What does this mean, my lady?"

"It's your special energy, lad, your electro-magnetism, you express it through your art—your music! It sings to you! It can tell you of the future. I have the gift, and you do too. So did my sweet Joshua, before he drowned aboard ship that horrible night thirteen years ago!"

Harriet turned on the light, and Roger put his clothes back on.

As the women put their robes back on, Roger looked at them for the first time with a trace of apprehension—and doubt. He shook his head, saying nothing, and left the cabin.

As he left, he didn't see First Officer Hamilton spying on him from around the corner.

Part Three:

"After the evening performance—which ends at ten sharp—you'll be confined to your third class quarters!" Potts wagged his beefy finger at Roger as he faced down the slim young musician in the conservatory, his breath blasting him with the usual unsavoury odours. "You've been warned not to create a disturbance, and now you pay the price!"

He had cornered Roger alone in the conservatory's huge closet where the instruments had been stored, the antagonists standing next to the formidable, wooden bass case. "The ship's Captain is not pleased with you, Roger my boy."

Potts moved closer to him, so that their bodies touched. His hungry eyes frisked Roger. "I see you're wearing the proper band uniform now. It looks very smart on you."

Potts smiled coldly, his yellow teeth displaying a piece of food wedged between his incisors. "You know Roger, perhaps I've been a bit hard on you."

The boy's eyes narrowed. "Do I play the bass tonight, sir?"

"Yes—and the trio in the small lounge near the library this morning, after Sunday chapel."

Potts ran his hand through Roger's thick, ginger-coloured hair.

Roger stepped back.

"Out of fairness," continued Potts, "you may bunk with me in my private, second-class cabin tonight if you wish. After all, this is the last night of the cruise."

Roger turned his back on Potts and attended to his bass instrument. "Yes, well, I'll think about it. In the mean time I'd better get cracking."

Potts marched away in a huff as Roger opened the case.

Turning his head back toward the departing bandleader, the lad watched the big man warily as he disappeared through the closet door.

"TALLULAH LIGHT-HANFORD ART EXHIBIT SUNDAY MORNING AT 10 AM AFTER CHAPEL SERVICE—A-DECK LIBRARY NEAR THE FORWARD STAIRCASE."

Roger, having finished his morning gig in the lounge, noticed the large sign standing near the ship's library as he made his way to his third class cabin. He detoured into the library, entering the spacious, mahogany-panelled room with the green-leather, padded chairs and the large porthole on the starboard side.

Potted palm trees dotted the rows of ornately decorated tables and crowded bookshelves. The porthole, about three feet in diameter and overlooking the calm ocean, allowed the nippy sea breeze to enter the room, causing the palm fronds to sway as if library occupied a tropical island.

Roger strolled past Tully's paintings--each labelled and named—on display in the library. He witnessed bright colours which at first seemed to clash, then gave one the feeling of an energetic new style.

The pieces contained all curved lines, which faded, and no straight lines. This imparted a sense of life's fluidity—that it's not definite. Seascapes, animals, buildings, with the odd portraits and figures, were represented.

Presently, Roger came upon two strange paintings on chest-high easels with gold frames. His eyes froze to the canvasses.

"Do you know what they are, Roger?"

Roger spun around, Tully's grave expression unnerving him. "No," he said in a subdued voice. "I don't"

"Roger, I can tell you're upset about last night. You're confused. You may doubt what you saw."

Roger just stared, his eyes glowing like a fine bottle of brandy resting in the sunlight. "Yes, I suppose I do."

"Trust Roger, trust! You must trust me!"

"Tell me about these paintings, Madame. These paintings here in the gold frames."

Upon one easel presented the image of a black bird with a yellow beak, its face savage and its beak covered in blood. The second easel showed a strange shape—what looked like a light brown pear that had been cut in half—opened and jointed at its centre, resting on a blue background.

"Let them speak to you, young man."

"I don't understand," said Roger.

"Think of what's ahead of you. Help me to save you, Roger!"

Roger's eyes flashed.

"What do you want me to do?"

"Meet me in my cabin at exactly midnight. Don't be late!" She clasped his hands in hers, her intense gaze burning through him. "Bring your bass instrument. It shall sing to us. Don't forget!"

"That'll be hard—"

"—Just do it!"

"I'll try."

"Don't try, do it! Your life may depend upon it!"

Roger, at first stunned, abruptly left the library. Tully watched him leave, shaking her head.

She walked slowly over to the porthole, the very cold wind hitting her in the face. No people had come yet to see her exhibit. Some said that there had been a whispering campaign against her all morning, reaching a fevered pitch at the Sunday service.

Tully stuck her head out the porthole. She stared at something in the water, caught in the ships wake. It sparkled in the morning sun.

It was a small piece of ice.

"Captain Smith, I want her out of first class, *now!*"

The phlegmatic captain, stroking his grey beard, fastened his stern, blue eyes upon the excited woman who had perched herself beside him, the deep wrinkles crinkling around his eyes. Prudence Smith had trapped him on the rear, port deck very close to the stern of the huge vessel.

"What would you have me do? The woman's already paid her thousand quid."

"I don't care! Put her in steerage if you have to. Must I put in a word with the owner?"

Her eyes drilled into the side of the captain's head as he looked out to sea. The distraught woman raised her voice to shrill. "I won't abide this woman any longer, do you understand? I've already discussed the situation with the chaplain this morning. We're in full agreement. She'll have no more rendezvous with that young boy, either!"

"I have a man on it. He'll handle it. We only have one more night—"

"—Just see that he does, Captain!"

"We'll think of something, *Madame*."

The late-afternoon sun set as the big ship glided at a fast clip through the still ocean, the sea almost as smooth as a millpond. The happy, first class passengers thronged the upper decks, getting in the last game of cards or shuffleboard. One passenger, who had been playing all day, pointed his paddle overhead at the curious sight over the forward funnel.

Other passengers gawked at the strange spectacle too, until a crowd had formed.

No one—even passengers who had crossed the North Atlantic dozens of times—had ever seen anything like it, especially this far out at sea. The men removed their hats, scratching their heads, as the women pointed to the oddity to show their children, not quite sure if they should be displaying such a strange incident to their sheltered brood.

A huge black bird circled in the air, diving at the billowing funnel, savagely smashing its sharp, yellow beak against the hot, mustard-coloured metal. It ascended, and dove again, crashing against hard targets on the vessel, as if trying to cripple it so that it would be forced to slow down.

The insane bird then aimed at passengers.

It circled, then swooped down, its scream shrill, its wings flapping frantically. Presently, it dove into a hat-rack, smashing its head against the blunt end of a hook. The bird lay on the first class deck stone dead, the yellow beak oozing blood, its black feathers tangled, its eyes fixed.

Roger Beacons, having just finished a trio engagement in the Fern Room, looked down at the motionless bird.

A flash of recognition registered in his eyes. He had seen the likeness of the bird before. Tully's painting had foretold the strange event! She had been right. She had been genuine, he realized.

Then, the rest of it must be true too.

He now trusted her completely.

He looked up to the sky, lost in thought. Somewhat stunned, he considered what this meant about him and what might happen to him, and then nodded to himself, as if he had just made up his mind.

Roger, exhausted from the strange voyage and his stressful work with Potts, had fallen asleep in his third class bunk, crammed in with another young man, a ship's mechanic from Wales.

As he wakened, he looked over at the small clock lying next to him. It was eleven-forty. He realized that something had caused him to wake up before his alarm had sounded—a strange noise.

Then, there were two thudding sounds, and a strange vibration, as if a giant—living in the sea—had rattled the ship in the clutches of its huge hands. Thinking nothing more of it, he jumped down from the bunk in his skivvies, turning on the small electric bulb that hung near the commode in the tiny compartment.

Careful not to wake his shipmate, he quietly dressed in his slacks, oxfords, and turtleneck sweater—with the red initials "W. S." sewn onto the right chest, an article of clothing that had been provided by the liner on his first night.

He quickly made his way to the thick metal door.

He had only fifteen minutes left to collect his bass instrument from the conservatory and present himself to Tully's first class cabin on the upper deck. He jiggled the knob—it didn't budge. He tried harder and it wouldn't open. He then pounded on the door. Still, nothing happened.

Roger realized that he had been locked in from the outside! He suspected that Potts had been responsible, perhaps in cahoots with the ships officers and that snooty society woman—Prudence Smith.

"That tiny old cabinet over there. You'll find a small air-duct grid behind it." Roger twisted toward the sound of the raspy voice, startled. "Remove that grid, and you can crawl out through the ventilation shaft to the centre hallway near the main exit."

Roger glanced into the lower bunk next to him. The voice had come from his roommate lying under the covers—the mechanic.

"Thank you," said Roger.

He rushed over to the cabinet lying against the wall and moved it, seeing the partially hidden grid. It looked just big enough for his slender body to squeeze through.

He reached into his pocket—removing a half-dollar coin—and jammed its edge into the crack between the grid and the frame. It separated enough for him to wedge his finger in, pulling it out from the wall enough to get his hand in.

He strained as hard as he could. Finally, the hard metal mesh came out from the frame. He threw it to the floor, and then fit his body through the small, square opening, just making it through.

Roger crawled through the dark shaft, hearing the squeaky sound of rats, their tiny feet patting against the metal. As he moved, he felt the sharp claws run over his legs.

He kicked the creatures away, and crawled faster. It was pitch black, and he could feel with his hand that he had come to a fork in the duct. Should he go right or left? He looked desperately for some clue as to which way to go, then—thinking that he heard something in the direction of the right turn—chose that one.

His knees hurting and his hands covered in filth, he finally came to another grid, which had light filtering in from the other side. He kicked it out, and then climbed through—only to find himself in the galley's garbage hold.

Wading though the likes of rotten banana peels and shelled lobster claws, he made for the door at the end of the room. Wiping the garbage off himself, he opened the door. He saw the main passageway leading to the tall, spiked exit-gate from third class to the bottom deck. A ship's steward was just locking the gate!

Then, fumbling with his keys, the steward snapped his fingers and frowned, obviously not finding the right key to lock the gate. He quickly left into the deck.

Roger ran through the gate and up the stairwell. He dashed to the conservatory and into the instrument closet, grateful to find that it had been left unlocked.

He quickly placed the huge bass— in its wooden case—on one of the strollers, and wheeled it out of the conservatory.

He pushed it quickly down the first class passageway, only to run into First Officer Hamilton, busy pounding on cabin doors about twenty yards ahead of him, his back turned. Roger quietly stepped to the turnoff to the door of Tully's cabin, the corner just five yards ahead, out of sight of Hamilton. He made it!

He figured that he was not too late, it most likely being just a little after midnight. Out of breath from his successful ordeal, he pounded on Tully's the door . . .

Tully, hearing the knocking on the cabin door, and figuring that Roger had kept the critical date after all, hugged Harriet. Both women, outfitted in casual but warm dresses, wore dour expressions.

"Go to the first class deck now, Harriet, and ready yourself."

"Yes, ma'am."

Tully looked around the cabin. The balcony door was open, letting in the freezing night air from the frigid North Atlantic. Champagne was resting on the coffee table, and the sound of Caruso—as Pinkerton in *Madame Butterfly*—crooned softly from the phonograph. Candles, rather than electric bulbs, burned throughout the room, their soft flicker instilling a sense of peace.

There was another pound on the door.

"Go now, Harriet." They hugged tightly.

Harriet opened the door and ushered Roger in, the young man pulling the instrument behind him. Harriet disappeared, shutting the door behind her.

Tully's eyes met Rogers. She moved very close to him, embracing him, running her fingers through his soft hair.

They danced very slowly, wrapped in each other's arms.

"Tully, the black bird with the yellow beak— it appeared—just as your painting said it would."

"Yes, my Roger."

"What does the bird mean?" Asked Roger in a trembling voice.

"What does your music mean, Roger?"

Roger, stunned, stopped the swaying rhythm of his dance. "I brought my bass, just as you requested."

Tully looked into Roger's eyes. "Set it up Roger, and play it for us. Let it sing to us."

"Yes."

He released her from his arms, and then moved over to his bass, lifting it off the transporter, and lugging it to the clear space by the balcony next to the glasses and champagne resting on the coffee table.

"While you're doing that Roger, I'll pour us some pink champagne."

"You look happy, Tully."

"I am. Soon, I'll be . . ."

Roger looked at Tully quizzically as he, straining, wrestled the huge case for his bass down on the floor next to his instrument. He then set up the towering instrument to play. He looked back at the balcony. "Maybe I should close the balcony door— it's chilly out there—"

"—No! Leave it be."

"Yes, ma'am."

Tully handed Roger a glass of champagne. They both drained their glasses. She took it from him, and she sat down by the table, pouring herself another.

"Now play."

Thunderous bangs upon the cabin door reverberated throughout the cabin. Tully glanced over at the entryway, waving the nuisance away. A man's muffled voice could be heard through the door. Tully ignored it.

Roger's head jerked in that direction.

"What's happening out there?"

"Forget it. It's probably one of Prudence Smith's baboons. Play!"

Roger played *Bach Cello Suite No. 1 for Double Bass, Prelude*—its sad, twisted, yet uplifting tune gripping Tully as no piece of music ever had. He played it in the lowest key possible, the volume generous.

Tully's eyes flowed with tears.

"It sings, Roger, what does it tell you?"

Roger stopped playing, his beautiful, brandy eyes taking on a dark cast. " . . . *Death*."

"The blackbird means death too," said Tully.

"I know—"

"There's no chance in third class Roger!" Tully put down her glass. "Stay close to your instrument!"

Roger put down his bow, his eyes shining with epiphany . . .

The ice-cold seawater crashed in through the balcony, sweeping Tully and Roger off their seats and slamming them against the far wall of the cabin.

Roger noticed the huge bass case hit the wooden floor, its metal latch breaking and the cedar case bursting open at its hinged joint.

To Roger, the salty water felt like thousands of needles piercing him at once, his breathing paralysed by the shock of its pounding, frigid force. As the cabin quickly filled with water, he heard Tully's voice, she screaming "Joshua, Joshua, Joshua! I'm *here* . . ."

Thrashing and flailing, tyring desperately to keep his mouth above the rising waterline, Roger's eyes searched for Tully, spotting her in the cabin's centre, bring sucked down in a whirlpool. Straining with all his might, he swam toward her, extending his nearly frozen hand to her.

He caught her collar, and yanked her too him, her cyanotic face just a few feet away. Their eyes met for just a second.

"Leave me be! I'm happy. Save yourself Roger! We hit an iceberg!"

Roger noticed that—amazingly—she had a look of bliss on her face.

Then, she was gone, disappearing beneath the swirling water. Almost as a reflex, Roger stroked as hard as he could toward the direction of his instrument, fighting to stay afloat. He could no longer feel his freezing legs scissoring in the water, his face being numb too. Just as he grabbed the handle of his case . . .

A huge, surging force clutched Roger's body and swept it through the balcony door, into the open North Atlantic. Roger, feeling frozen and lifeless, his senses blunted, experienced the violence of the catastrophe in what seemed like slow motion.

It was as if he were outside of himself, watching one of those funny nickelodeon picture shows at the carnival.

He saw flashes of things before him, his struggling mind barely able to piece them together to make a story of what was happening to him. He turned his head around, catching the site of the huge ship, a slight list from bow to stern, sitting upon the water. It gave the appearance of—with its rows of bright lights still burning in a moonless sky—a shiny, safe island in a dark abyss.

He thought he heard the sound of the band playing.

No, that can't be!

All of a sudden, an overwhelming, sucking force yanked his body down, down, down deep into the cold darkness, as chairs, tables, bodies, and other flotsam escaped to the surface, thrashing him along the way. He felt no pain, just the pressure of these projectiles hitting his body again and again.

Then, he noticed a flash of bright light in the bubbling, glittering water, accompanied by the eardrum-splitting force of an explosion. The water around him became even murkier and larded with debris. Perhaps one of the huge boilers had exploded, he realized.

I'm going to die now.

Preparing to drown—expecting these seconds on earth to be his last—Roger quickly rushed through his manner of prayer as he felt his lungs bursting from lack of air. He could not longer hold his breath, and he was losing consciousness.

All of a sudden, another blast had propelled his body back up to the surface, like a little doll being tossed around in a draining bathtub.

He could feel his head emerge from the water, the freezing night air filling his starving lungs as he gasped and coughed to clear his airway. He opened his stinging eyes and looked around, seeing all manner of objects floating about him, including countless bodies of men, women, and children—most still and face down.

Yet, in the background, he could faintly hear music playing.

The clothing of these drowned people, he had oddly noticed in his panic, was not the fine garb of the privileged. Roger, paddling frantically in the swirling, rippling water, then heard a shrill sound coming from above.

He looked up.

A huge, metal, mustard-coloured object crashed down upon him. He swam away as hard as he could, most of his strength having left him. The giant, cylindrical mass slammed against the water next to him, just missing his head by yard. At least a dozen men, before thrashing and kicking in the water, had been crushed by one of the ship's gigantic funnel smokestacks.

Roger swam for his life, frantically trying to get away from the remnants of the sinking vessel, and all the dying passengers and dangerous debris that went with it. To his astonishment, the surface became almost as smooth as glass as he gained more distance.

And again, he could hear music playing.

He scanned the surface for signs of life, or keys to his salvation. Sleep gripped him like a soothing hand, giving him a false sense of wellbeing. The ice cold completely exhausted him, sapping his will to live. He realized that very soon he would be dead, just like all the others.

I'm tired—I just want to go to sleep.

A white lifeboat glided past him in the water. He glanced at the passengers, all four of them in that boat, bundled warmly in wool blankets and winter minks.

All of a sudden, his eyes momentarily met the harsh stare of Prudence Smith, as she turned her head away and looked in the other direction. Roger, too weak to call out, just waved, but it was no use. First Officer Hamilton just kept oaring, leaving him behind to his fate.

Next, Potts, wearing his life jacket that was way too small for him, floated by like some lifeless blue whale, his eyes round and unblinking in death.

Roger grabbed in desperation for bits and pieces of objects floating near, none suitable to assist his quest to stay alive. He rotated in the water, looking behind him, as he gulped water, not having the strength to keep his head above the surface any longer.

He heard the music again. It came from the fantail—the last part of the great vessel still above the surface, dark and sinking, the remaining passengers clinging to its surface like so many ants on a log being drowned by a garden hose.

The music, realized Roger, was the band playing "Near My Lord to Thee", and then it went silent. The fantail disappeared beneath the surface, not two hundred yards away, as the shrill screams of the passengers went silent as well.

Just as Roger gulped another mouthful of water, and was about to go down, his dulled eyes greeted the object of his salvation floating by with a rapture of which he thought he was no longer capable.

At the sight of it, his mind flashed with the recollection of a similar image in one of Tully's paintings foretelling the future: the pear-like brown object—cut in half—its parts still partially joined at the centre.

It looks just like her picture!

Floating in the water, Roger Beacons saw his huge, wooden bass case—like a lifeboat sent from the Almighty—wide open and welcoming, just big enough to fit his slight torso into one half, and his slender legs in the other!

With his remaining strength, and tapping all his remaining willpower, and slowly pulled his exhausted and nearly frozen body into the small vessel, its buoyancy just adequate to keep him afloat.

At that moment, he thought about his special gift, and his guardian angel—Tully. He had a lot to be thankful for.

It was then, at the moment of defying certain death, that he noticed the small, wooden sign float by—a piece of the icon of the age of reason—gloating about the final triumph of humankind and science over nature.

"WELCOME TO THE UNSINKABLE RMS TITANIC!"

END

Epilogue

With the dulling of our imaginations and the innocence of childhood as we age, do we lose something powerful and special as well? Make-believe can be powerful, and life's stress and trials rob many of us of that uncanny ability to find their "quiet and special place". The little girl in Novelette One tried to help her parents, but only one of them could be helped. The mother had therefore been left behind, as many of us would be.

Much has been written about the "banality" of evil, but what about the "sexiness" of evil—which is much more interesting. Like it or not, the youthful Adolf Hitler in Novelette Two was indeed, by most contemporary accounts, alluring and attractive—and devilishly personable when he wanted to be. The photograph snapped by the fictional character at the end of Novelette Two represented a famous, real-life photo that was taken of a twenty-five year old Hitler on August 2, 1914, in Munich's Odeon's Square, celebrating the new war with Russia. To this day it generates controversy. What happened before and during the carnage of WW 1 that helped transform "Audi"—a nickname he actually used—into the monster he later became—something like the story?

Death in Venice on a cruise-ship" is how one could think of Novelette Three, but that's too ambitious a comparison with Thomas Mann's great novella. However, the link between the sensual, spiritualistic, and the disintegration of our minds in old age is a worthy topic, and lessons might be learned. The mystical nymph Roger is one bright shadow that could have been in the Titanic band.

www.ingramcontent.com/pod-product-compliance
Lightning Source LLC
Chambersburg PA
CBHW060257150626
46556CB00021B/927